I0631009

AURACLE

DAWN MOSSMAN

First published in 2016
By Dawn Mossman d.b.a Vera Wellner

Copyright © 2016
Dawn Mossman

A revised version
This edition published 2019

2nd revised version
This edition published 2022

Editor
Tim Covell, Somewhat Grumpy Press

Illustrator
Christian Bentulan, Covers By Christian

Photo Credit
Roberta Smith

ISBN
978-0-9958121-3-0

authordmossman@gmail.com

This book is dedicated to the medical community, especially the staff from the IWK and Nova Scotia Cancer Centre.

CHAPTER 1

Mom was rushing around our kitchen getting a bottle and cereal ready for my baby sister, Mara. Dad was sitting in his usual spot at the kitchen table, facing the door to the porch. He was drinking a cup of tea and eating a biscuit with molasses, an old Maritime favorite. The radio was tuned to the country station.

"It's our third consecutive day with record temperature highs. The winter of 2002 is looking like it will be our warmest yet." The radio announcer said.

Mom and Dad weren't getting ready, they don't work during the winter months. They work at the seafood processing plant. It opens May first and shuts down at the end of the fishing season in October. I love having them at home, but money gets tight when they are on employment insurance. I know not to ask for much during the winter.

I threw some bread in the toaster, scarfed down a bowl of Cheerios and ate my toast with strawberry jam. I finished with a tall glass of orange juice. I made a sour face from the tartness of the jam mixed with the juice.

The day started the same way as every Wednesday morning in the winter. Four months later, I am amazed at how much has changed.

"Okay guys, I've got to run! I don't want to leave Nila waiting for me." I grabbed my school bag and headed for the door. "Have a great day!"

"Bye Violet. You too!" My parents replied in unison.

I met my best friend, Nila, as she was walking on the path we had worn between our houses. We live on the same block. My house is on the front of the block and her house is behind, facing the other street. She has been my best friend forever, my BFF. We grew up together in our neighborhood. I am happy we live so close. I love her to death, and I enjoy her company more than anyone else's. We are kindred spirits. We just seem to belong together.

"Hey Nila, ready for another thrilling day at Glencarter Junior High?" I sighed.

"Yeah right, Vi," Nila replied.

We were in the ninth grade and looking forward to starting senior high school next year. We were super excited but a little scared, too. Meanwhile, this was our year to rule the junior high school. We'd waited for this since seventh grade, but so far this year had been a complete bust.

Our school has the elementary grades on one side of the building and the junior high grades on the other side. Each set of grades have their own entrance and floor inside the building, and separate exits to the playground at the back. A large cement wall divides the playground area between the younger kids and the older ones. The older grades hang out there during breaks or lunch hour when it's nice outside.

We were finally the oldest kids in junior high. No one was bullied by the older kids – we were the older kids. Other than that, not much had changed. I was looking forward to March Break and some time away from early mornings, homework, and school.

Nila was walking ahead of me on the path, and she kept tugging at the waist of her skinny jeans. Her tummy was spilling out over the top of them. Although she'd recently lost a few pounds, people might say the style was not the most suitable for her. I would never tell her that. I'm sure it would hurt her feelings. Nila's been bullied for years because of her weight. The people who tease her don't seem to notice her beautiful face and great hair. Awesome hair! It's raven with hints of blue when the sun catches it the right way. Nila has darker features, thanks to her Mi'kmaq ancestry. And most important, she has a huge heart.

The kids in our classes never bothered her much. I think they knew how generous she was, and they mostly gave the girl a much-deserved break. She's also one of the best players on our girl's school basketball team.

The walk to school was about ten minutes with the short-cuts we took. We walked across lawns and cut through people's driveways. We had no shame about it either. No one seemed to mind much except for one old bag on the second corner. Every time she caught us, she opened her window and yelled at us to get the hell off her lawn.

We took the old train tracks from Church Hill Street directly to the road the school is on. This was the last of our many short-cuts. The trains stopped running years ago. The only one I can remember seeing here was a two-car cargo train that stopped at the potato warehouse close to our school.

The train was the first thing to stop operating in Glencarter. Since then, a lot of processing plants and businesses have either gone bankrupt or burned down. Nila and I imagine that one day Glencarter will be nothing but a ghost town or maybe a tourist resort.

There are already a lot of tourists. There are plenty of ocean beaches around here too. And you can get lots of privacy, unless you're a local, then you get very little. But if you are from away and privacy is your thing, then Glencarter may be your ideal Atlantic seaside retreat. During the summer months, Glencarter has tons more traffic than the rest of the year. Shiny new vehicles drive all over town with license plates from other provinces in Canada and from all over the United States.

The winter months are a different story. It's quiet, and there is not much to do other than go to the cinema on the weekend to see a movie or watch a hockey game at the rink.

Nila and I chatted about the week's events as we walked.

"I saw on Facebook, our school won the hockey game last night. Rusty scored three goals and was the star of the game." Nila announced, while pulling up her waistband.

I wasn't surprised. He was the star almost every game. He dared to make plays no one else would, but that's Rusty.

"I'm sure he will be Male Athlete of the Year at our graduation." I said. "No one else in our class comes close to him, not at sports anyways, and looks." I laughed.

He looked good playing sports, and not only because he was a skilled athlete. He was pretty damn dreamy, and the most popular boy in our school.

"Rusty will win for sure," Nila agreed. "I hate to say it, but I thought he was totally out of our league, Ambers too."

We were talking more than usual about Rusty because he asked Amber out, and she was going to the movies with him that weekend.

Amber is our other best friend, the third and last member of our trio. She was super stoked that Rusty had asked her out. And why shouldn't she be? I had secretly thought he was totally out of Amber's league too.

Amber was waiting for us, like she did most mornings, at a bench just inside the main doors. It's close to the cafeteria, which was where most of the kids hung out during breaks and lunch hour when the weather was cold. We often sat there to talk and watch people going to and fro. Amber looked up from her phone and smiled at us as we walked toward the bench.

"Hello girls!" Amber cheerfully almost sang us a greeting as we met. Her blonde curls danced about her shoulders as she turned toward us.

Amber looked great. Amber always looked great. She was wearing a fitted gray jacket with stretchy dark denim jeans that accentuated her figure, and a pair of high black leather riding boots that are a favorite of mine. I've always been a tad jealous of Amber.

Her complexion is fair, and she has a few freckles across her nose that are most prominent in the summer. Her soft blonde hair hangs in long loose waves that crash about with her bubbly personality. She sounds like she sings when she speaks. What more can I say? It's no wonder Rusty asked her out.

Amber's dad calls her Princess. It suits her. He has always called her that. I remember when we were in elementary school, he would drop her off. A couple of the boys in our class heard him calling her Princess. They started calling Amber "Little Prissy Princess Pants or Lil P's for short." I think it was mostly Alex but ever since then, Amber's dad is not allowed to call her Princess in public.

Amber is a year older than the rest of our class. She failed the first grade. I believe the only reason the girl failed was because she wanted to be in the same class as Nila and me. Amber could be a bit flaky, sure thing, but the girl is certainly no dummy. She has always been book smart.

Physically, I am light-years behind Amber. I haven't developed much at all. I am by far the shortest of us three girls. Nila is at least three inches taller than me and though she carries her weight well, her shape is more or less round.

I was surprised that Amber hadn't ditched us. She still hung around with two plain Janes like me and Nila. It's true we all grew up together on the same block, but Amber's family came into money. They moved to the better side of town, while Nila and I are still stuck in the dreaded lower end of Glencarter.

"Hi Amber, yo-gonna ever return my yoga video?" I asked. It was my lame attempt at a pun. I had loaned Amber the tape two weeks ago. She borrowed it to burn and was supposed to return it right after. It was not a big deal, but it had been two weeks and I did want it back. Amber's abundance of beauty sometimes seemed balanced by a lack of common sense. Like I said before, she was book smart, but she could be flaky.

"Sorry Violet, I forgot it at home… again. Blonde moment! Tomorrow, I promise."

"I won't hold you to it." I laughed.

The first bell rang. The three of us walked into English class and headed for our seats. Our seats were on the far side of the room, near the windows. We watched as Rusty and his buddies, Alex and Craig, busted in through the classroom door. Alex and Craig have been his best friends since grade school.

Rusty really is quite the specimen. His muscular athletic frame is complimented by brown wavy hair and dark brown eyes. I may have referred to him as tall, dark, and handsome in the past.

Alex is a little shorter than Rusty with blond hair and blue eyes. He makes up for his smaller build with a huge voice that bellows up from deep within. He can be heard above everyone else in a crowd and he is the first to holler out something smart-assed or stupid for a good laugh. Alex has a reputation for fighting, especially after a couple of beers.

Craig is the opposite. He is quieter and skinnier than Alex and Rusty, but much brighter. He is just as sporty. I think that his light weight must help him with his speed because he is fast, almost as fast as Rusty, and almost as agile too. Craig doesn't seem to know everyone like Alex and Rusty do, although all three of them are popular kids in this town.

Craig has a small scar at the top of his hairline along the left side of his face. Some people say it was from a fight. I've heard others say it was caused by a skateboarding accident. Since I'd never heard of him fighting, or seen him with a skateboard, neither made sense. I was curious, but not enough to be asking popular boys about their scars.

Rusty took his seat on the other side of Amber's. He smiled at her as he sat down at his desk. Amber couldn't help but smile back at him, and who wouldn't? It was Rusty. I watched as her smile quickly turned to a frown when Ruby walked into our classroom. Ruby was Rusty's girlfriend for a couple of months. They first dated back in elementary, if you could even call it that, but she's carried a flame for him ever since. They started dating again this year, but he broke up with her a few weeks ago. His excuse was that he wasn't looking for anything serious, bad timing. It was big news. Everyone heard all about it. Ruby glared at Amber as she took her seat directly behind Rusty. Amber looked away.

Ruby is the youngest in her family. Her father is the mayor of Glencarter. He has always worked for the city. He used to oversee the low rentals in the lower end before he ran for office. He played sports when he was younger. He's famous here for scoring the winning goal during a legendary gold medal provincial midget hockey game for Glencarter against Georgetown back in 1990. Ruby looks a lot like him.

She has red hair and green eyes. She is a pretty ginger and she is tall, like her brothers. Her three older brothers helped pave the way for her at school and in town. They are well-liked and great at hockey and soccer. Ruby is just as athletic and popular as they are. Courtesy of her family gene pool, I guess. She's never been smart, but with her physical capabilities, looks, and family name, you don't need brains, at least not in this town.

Ruby's always been into sports. Her family could afford it, and she grew up playing alongside her brothers. So yes, Ruby's an athlete, and she thought she had won the grand prize when she and Rusty were dating. She wanted him back. Ruby had absolutely no qualms letting Amber know it, or making her life miserable in the process.

The second bell rang, for classes to begin.

"Good morning class," Mrs. Walker began, "Time for attendance."

The room was buzzing as Mrs. Walker tried to get through the roll call. Everyone was present, including Beryl. Beryl is Ruby's best friend. She's not the athletic type like Ruby, but better than others like me. Beryl is the intellectual type. She must have the highest IQ score in our school. Beryl is also gorgeous, with long dark brown hair and deep blue eyes. Although she is smart and better looking than Ruby, she's a follower, not a leader, and she did not mind taking a back seat to Ruby. I think that's why they get along so well. Beryl is not as outgoing or bold as Ruby and could be attentive and deferential when she wanted to be. Most of our teachers favored her over the rest of us.

And then there's Perry. Four months ago, I thought Perry was just–how do I put this politely? Peculiar, and probably a little creepy too. He always had been. He was smart, in this own way, I suppose. But he did not fit the mold here in Glencarter, in anything. He sucked at sports and he kept to himself. In the first and second grade he had a lot of imaginary friends. Sometimes he acted like he still had them. He would blurt something strange out of nowhere in the middle of class, or whisper to himself. Even among the junior high freaks and geeks, he stood out.

Mrs. Walker adjusted her glasses as she opened her copy of *Where the Red Fern Grows*. We took out our copies.

"Beryl, please begin reading where we last left off, page one hundred and two. As for the rest of the class, please follow along in your copies. Thank you!"

"Thank you, Mrs. Walker," said Beryl. She started reading.

"So Rusty," I heard Ruby whisper, "we are playing a game of touch football this Saturday afternoon. My brothers would love to see you there. Any chance you might be interested in coming? Maybe afterwards we can go out for hot chocolate or something."

The winter had been on the mild side. We hardly had any snow, but with two weeks left until March Break the ground was still frozen and too hard for tackle football.

"Sorry Ruby," Rusty replied. "I'm busy Saturday." Rusty smiled and looked over at Amber.

Amber's face turned red from embarrassment. Ruby's face turned red in anger. There will be trouble at lunch, I thought.

CHAPTER 2

Nila, Amber, and I carried our lunch trays over to our usual table in the cafeteria, close to the stage. The cafeteria is where we hold our school assemblies and dances. It has an audio system that some of the senior class students are allowed to use during lunch hour. Alex and Craig were manning the system that day, and The Tragically Hip was playing.

I had a large order of fries with ketchup and a soda. I am a picky eater. I don't go for the lunch specials. So, this wasn't a tough decision for me. It's always between the fries, a cold plate or, if I am trying to save money, a bagel. Nila and Amber each got the specials. It was meatloaf again. Yuck! Our options weren't great food, but we were hungry and got right to eating. Who eats meatloaf anymore? The people of Glencarter, that's who!

The white cafeteria walls are plastered with posters from different committees requesting help or promoting upcoming events. There's the Chess Club, the Future Farmers, and 4-H, just to name a few.

Sometimes we seem light-years behind the times. Glencarter is a rural, backwoods, small town. It's the type of town where everyone knows everyone and all their business. There are tons of old folklore stories from generations past. Some people scrape by making a bare living from the land or sea, like my parents, while others have cushy jobs thanks to family connections. Glencarter is named after the most prominent family from the area, the Carter's. There are tons of them here, but Glen was not one of them. Not that I know of anyways. Glen was not a person, but a place.

The Glen is on the outskirts of town. The land was claimed by some of the early Europeans who came to this area. They tried to farm and form a colony there, but the soil is poor. A few took up fishing and moved closer to the water. The rest eventually moved on and abandoned the original settlement. A few decades ago, property speculators from away put in dirt roads for a subdivision, some signs, and set up a few trailers for sales offices. Nothing came of it.

What was left is a maze of dirt roads among closely spaced tall trees. They line both sides of the roads and meet overhead. It is a stunning drive in the summer and fall, and it's always shady. It's a good way to avoid the summer heat. The roads are impossible to drive most winters except by snowmobile, but this winter we had hardly any snow.

Most of the older kids from Glencarter hang out in The Glen to party. Tourists don't know The Glen exists, and it's an easy way to avoid the police. They don't travel the dirt roads, not around here anyways. If the roads are not paved, I guess it's considered too much in the sticks to worry about.

There are a few camps that people use for hunting and for tapping maple syrup. Rusty's family owns one of the sheds there. His family uses it for harvesting maple syrup. Rusty and his older brother hang out there most weekends with their friends and friends of friends. Everyone calls it The Sugar Shack.

Ruby and Beryl's laughing distracted me from thoughts of Rusty and The Sugar Shack. Ruby's clique was sitting at the lunch table in front of ours. Then I saw what they were laughing about.

"Ruby, you shouldn't." Beryl snickered as a piece of cinnamon roll landed in Amber's hair. The other girls at their table laughed, and Ruby tossed another piece.

"Hey Princess," Ruby shouted, "How's your reign?"

The play on words was clever, if cruel. Beryl must have come up with it. Ruby could not have thought of it on her own.

Amber was humiliated! She didn't have the guts to go up against Ruby, and this made her an easy target. Amber receives lots of positive attention, with her sunny disposition and good looks. But she is not good at handling negativity. She cowers from confrontation and Ruby knows it.

It's something we have in common. I am one of the quieter kids in class. It's not that I didn't want to say anything. I did. But I was scared I'd be bullied too.

Amber was fighting hard to hold back tears. Ruby's friends were laughing louder, and other students were looking to see what was so funny. I looked at Nila. It really wasn't in her nature to say something either. We stood up, unsure what to do. There was a noisy crash to our right. Bang! Dishes clattered. Everyone stopped and turned to see what happened. It was Perry. He had dropped his lunch tray.

"Sorry," he apologized. He was speaking softly, as if to himself. "Thought I caught something out of the corner of my eye." His voice faded out as he bent down and picked up his lunch.

That was weird, but useful. The distraction held Amber back from a complete breakdown in the middle of the crowded cafeteria. She jumped up and fled out to the hall. Nila and I followed close behind her.

"Ruby is nothing but a small-minded slug and you know the bitch is just jealous!" I tried to reassure Amber.

I looked over to Nila for help. She was close to tears herself.

"I know," Amber replied as we walked the empty corridor. She sounded defeated. "I cannot believe what a bully she can be! Do you think I should cancel my date with Rusty? You know this is all over him. She's been glaring at me since Rusty asked me out, and I don't know if I can handle much more. What's next? Is she going to beat me up? You know that girl is strong, and she'll have lots of backup too!"

I knew Amber was right about that. Ruby would have lots of people to take her side and back her up in a fight. Ruby has lots of older friends from her brother's connections and some girls in our class would use any opportunity to get in with the cool kids. Ruby was not the most likable kid in our class, but she was one of the most popular. I didn't want Amber to back out of her date though, and Nila felt the same way.

"Don't cancel, Amber," Nila begged. "If you do, we won't blame you but please don't." Nila's voice lifted. "I would love to see someone, especially you, get one over on Ruby for a change." Amber smiled. "If you cancel, then she wins again. You will be giving her exactly what she wants, rewarding her." Nila was trying hard to persuade Amber. "And that's the last thing we want!"

We all laughed at that.

"You're right," said Amber. "I'm going with Rusty, despite Ruby."

CHAPTER 3

After homework, supper, and the six o'clock news, I sat with my family in our living room. Our living room is like the rest of the house, small but cozy. The walls are old wood paneling, and the floor is hardwood. We don't have much furniture in our living room. There is not enough room for it. We have a velveteen couch and a large chair that came together as a set. There is also a big gray recliner Dad has claimed as his.

That evening, Mara was playing on a blanket Mom had spread out for her in front of the couch. I liked watching her play.

When Nila and I were small, both of us had wished for a little sister or brother. We imagined them like little dolls I suppose, our own "real babies." I was ecstatic when Mom said she was pregnant. I'd secretly wished for a girl, and I was happy as a clam at high tide when Mom had Mara. Living with a baby and having a sister was not like I'd expected. There is a thirteen-year age difference between us. I don't want a baby of my own anymore and I end up having to babysit most weekends even when I don't want to because I already have plans of my own. Technically Nila has her little brother now too, since her dad had a kid with his new girlfriend. But it's hard to include him in the count since she hardly ever sees him or her dad.

We were lounging around the living room watching *The Big Bang Theory*. I was strung across the arms of the big chair as Mara practiced rolling around and sitting up on her blanket. I marveled as I watched her manage yoga poses.

"Mom, soon Mara is going to be better at yoga than I am!" So far, she's conquered "the happy baby" which may not be that impressive on its own, since she's a baby, but now she is learning "downward facing dog."

Mara was on all fours, trying to straighten her back legs.

"She is just trying to figure out how to get up and around on her own, Violet. She's not doing yoga yet." Mom said.

I still could not help but be impressed by her abilities.

As we sat there together, I had the strange feeling of déjà vu. It's when everything around you seems familiar, like you've lived this moment before. Watching TV with my parents was nothing new, but everything with Mara was new. Perhaps I had dreamed this, I thought. It was not my first time experiencing déjà vu, but it had never been so strong.

Nan, my grandmother, told me that when she had déjà vu, something big would happen in her life shortly afterward. She taught me all sorts of cool stuff. She taught me the value of prayer and meditation. They are good for the soul, and they help you to relax or to settle you to sleep. I can be a bit of a nervous Nelly. Nan gave me a set of tuning forks for my eighth birthday, to help calm me down. She said to sit cross-legged and clang them together around me three times, once at each of my sides and the last time over my head. The vibration from the forks is supposed to help me tune my own energy with the frequency of energy around me, something like tuning a piano. I don't know how it works, but I always feel better afterwards. Do not get me wrong, I would die of embarrassment if someone else saw me do this. I know they would think I'd completely lost it.

Nan was the matriarch of our family. My mom and I turned to her for all sorts of help and guidance. Most of it came down to general advice. I spent the majority of my weekends with her. Sometimes I would bring Nila or Amber with me. They called my grandmother Nan too. She was warm and had a soothing manner. She had a wicked sense of humor, and she got a kick out of listening to us kids laugh and carry on.

Nan died three years ago from cancer. She went through chemo and radiation treatments as long as her body could handle them. Eventually she didn't have the strength to eat anymore.

When she was healthy, she lived alone, and my grandfather died before I was born. She lived in a small two-story house up east of Glencarter. The house is like ours and a lot of the other older houses in the area. Hers had an extension built on at the back that included a small porch and a laundry room. My parents sold her house shortly after she died. They said it was to pay for her funeral and to get caught up on some of our bills. I begged them not to sell it, not to give it up. I didn't want to lose anymore of Nan. My opinion didn't matter and now the only thing we have from the sale of her place are a few small things and a car that will probably rust out before I finish high school.

For the first two years after Nan died, I dreamed about her a lot. In my dreams, Nan and I were mostly in the back bedroom of her house. That was odd, because since I was five, I slept in the front bedroom. Nan had bad arthritis and she didn't leave the house much the last few years before she'd passed. She had arthritis and said the pavement hurt her feet. She spent those years of her life sleeping downstairs in the living room. She found it too hard to take the stairs, so she preferred to stay on the main floor. She had a day bed set up in her living room that doubled as her sofa during the day. That house was where she lived and where she died.

In my dreams, I did know that her house had been sold and that someone else owned it. The new owners always let us stay in the house as guests. I never saw them. I just knew there was an arrangement and even though the house was theirs now, we were welcome to stay as long as Nan wanted or until she died, whichever came first. It was kind of ironic considering she was already dead.

I wasn't surprised when I heard that the new owners of Nan's house said the place was haunted. I wanted to ask them if the activity was coming from the back bedroom of the house at night. I convinced myself that my dreams were true, and our spirits reunited every night at Nan's. I think she chose the back room out of respect for the new owners who were kind enough to let her stay.

When Mom had Mara, the dreams stopped. I told myself it was because Nan could finally be at rest, knowing I have Mara. Not that I didn't need her anymore, but I had someone new that I could love and turn my attention to. I want to teach Mara the wisdom Nan had passed onto me.

Mara started working on a new pose. It resembled the cobra. I got down on the floor beside her, to demonstrate, but she started giggling, so we rolled around on the floor.

If I ever get up the nerve, I will be asking the new owners of Nan's house if the activity in their home has stopped and if it happened at the same time my little sister was born. I have a feeling they will remember the date.

CHAPTER 4

Later that night, lying in bed, I thought about Amber and Nila. On our way home from school, Nila confided in me that she wished she could do more for Amber. She hated to see her hurting. That's Nila's way. Even though Amber was one of our best friends, she would have felt the same way for almost anyone. Unfortunately, there was not much we could do to help. Ruby didn't care about us or what *we* wanted.

Another lackluster day in the lower end. The place where dreams develop in plenty, but nothing ever lasts, and no one amounts to much of anything.

The lower end is my part of town. It's where most of the people with lower incomes live. Some families are in their own modest homes, often passed down from one generation to the next, like ours. It belonged to my dad's family, and it was passed down to him. His parents moved to the island from Newfoundland when Glencarter was booming. He was born and raised here. His parents moved back after businesses started closing here, and work became scarce. Dad decided to stay, and he took over the house. It's a small, peaked house with neutral tan wooden shingles and green trim. My parents painted it about five years ago. I guess they like it because they haven't changed the color or done much with it since, or maybe they can't afford to. The color is bland for my taste, but it's coordinated with most of the houses on our block.

A lot of the other houses are low rentals. At least, that's what they are called here. Low rentals are duplexes or semis the government built about twenty years ago. The exteriors of the two and three-story buildings are beige, and they look nice from the outside, for the neighborhood, though worn. Every house has a maple tree in the front yard. The insides are plain, with cheap carpets, and the kitchen cabinets are falling apart.

Many of the low rentals are occupied by single parents, mostly mothers, who rent the property from the government for a percentage of their income. It is usually cheaper than paying a private landlord, and often in no worse condition. With all the single parents, a lot of the kids from the neighborhood don't have their dads, or moms, around much.

I am one of the lucky few who have both of my parents living at home with me. Nila, not so much. Her father was a deadbeat and he left when she was six. He lives in a different town now. His new girlfriend is only ten years older than Nila. When Nila's brother was born, they wanted Nila to feel included in their new family. She thought he was trying to make up for lost time. It's been about a year or two since she spoke to her dad, and she doesn't know her little brother at all.

Amber got out of the lower end. Her mom and dad were off and on when we were little, and her dad drank a lot. Then he was lucky enough to inherit a fishing fleet from a relative, an uncle who'd passed away with no children of his own. Her dad had been a deckhand on his uncle's boat since he was a teenager, so it only seemed fit that he was left the fleet. Amber was ten at the time and her parents got married soon after they received his portion of the estate. The result was Amber's family finding their way out of the lower end, tout de suite. Amber's parents are great people, who do genuinely care for her, but Amber is able to get away with much more than Nila and I ever can.

Amber's dad still drinks a lot. The lower end isn't just a home for poverty. There is also addiction – mostly alcohol and marijuana. We notice the alcohol more with the older men on the block. There are a handful of old men who most times you wouldn't even know drink but occasionally, about as often as the seasons change, go on a binge. You don't see it coming but I have the feeling they do, and from deep down within their bones, like arthritis setting in from the rain. Then the day comes when a few of them sit around and decide today is the time to have a drink. One drink leads to another and then a couple more and so on and so forth. The drinking continues until all their money is gone, and they've completely drained their resources. Then they head to the detox center to dry out.

Some of the younger parents seem to favor marijuana, maybe to avoid the hangovers, I'm not sure. One way or another, we have grown up around addiction. It's all around us. It's just the way of life in the lower end. There's a lot of trouble here, and in lots of other places too.

I needed to get to sleep. I always try to either pray or meditate before I go to sleep at night, as they help calm me down and relax for sleep. My prayer is not the traditional church prayer. It's simply me saying hello or I'm thankful for the blessings in my life. Although, I do find myself asking for help more often than I like to admit but I think most people do that.

Almost everyone in Glencarter is Catholic, including me, but my family doesn't attend church much. I had to go to Sunday school until the end of seventh grade. After I was confirmed, I was allowed to quit. My confirmation present from my parents. When my family rarely does go, we always sit at the back. Mom says the people at our church are more concerned about gossip than the gospel. The congregation likes to talk about who is there, what they are wearing, and who is living in sin. Mom tries to avoid it all together. She doesn't see it as a celebration of Christ.

My meditation isn't traditional either. I lie down and try to clear my mind of thought while taking slow deep breaths. I focus on my breathing. Sometimes I concentrate on a speck of light I imagine inside of my third eye. Nan told me the light will release impurities from my body as it grows. The light starts in the center of my forehead and slowly seeps down. Eventually the light will flow out from the top of my head through my body and shoot from the bottom of my feet. Any negativity leaves with the light and you are left with an improved sense of well-being.

That night, I chose prayer, given the day's events.

God, you see and know everything. Please help guide me so I can help my friend Amber. Amen.

After I asked for clarity on what I could for Amber, I soon fell into a deep sleep. I was being lifted quickly rising higher, warm air against my skin. Colors soared with me. I saw red, orange, yellow, green, blue, indigo, and violet, the same colors of the rainbow. My insides grew warmer and warmer the higher I went. I became happier and happier with the rising heat.

I heard a girl's voice calling me. "Violet… Violet… Violet… It's your time." I didn't recognize the voice, and normally I would be nervous about meeting someone new, but my instinct was to find the source. She sounded my age. I looked around for her, but the voice got fainter and it got darker as the colors faded.

Even though we didn't meet that night, I was still reassured. I sensed that she was kind, and her message was good.

CHAPTER 5

Thursday, we had Phys. Ed. First thing. It was the class I dreaded most. I was not gifted with any athletic ability whatsoever. Neither was Amber, but at least she looked good attempting to play sports. That was more than I could say.

I admired her gym class attire. Amber always wore nice clothes. That morning she wore a hot pink tank top with short black polyester Under Armour shorts. The outfit flattered her figure. Amber's dad bought her the coolest black sneakers from the Nike store in the city. When she first wore them to gym class, Nila and I almost died with envy. She complements them with bright yellow laces. It's her favorite color.

Amber was in a chipper mood, and I was surprised, given yesterday's run-in with Ruby. Amber smiled at me, and I could not help but smile back. Her happy mood was infectious as always.

"Good morning," Mr. Lavie announced, as he began the class. Mr. Lavie was a star athlete when he was a student here at the junior high and in high school. He earned a sports scholarship and he attended university in the city. He's in his late twenties or early thirties now, tall, handsome, still athletic, and most of the girls have a major crush on him. "We're going to warm up this morning with five laps. Let's get started!" Mr. Lavie began running. The class followed behind him. The boys and Ruby were in the front, the rest of us in the rear. We started together but after a few minutes we were spread out around the perimeter of the gym.

Amber, Nila, and I ran together. The different colored lines on the wooden gym floor, for various sports, reminded me of my dream. The walls, made of oversized concrete blocks, were painted white. We ran past a set of wooden bleachers that extended the length of the gym. Above them, a large painting of our school mascot, a pirate, looked over the gym. As usual, it smelled like a dirty laundry basket in there. I hated the smell of the gym. Craig, the fastest in our class, lapped us as we talked.

"So, we're getting close to my big date night, girls." Amber looked at me, then over to Nila.

"I know," Nila agreed. "I think you guys will definitely hit it off. I wish he was in the afternoon gym class. I'd like to watch him work up a sweat. Il est si beau!" Nila wiped her brow and shook her hand in the air, as if she was shaking the sweat off of it. "You're gorgeous, he's gorgeous! You'd make a perfect pair! As long as he doesn't act like a complete ass, and well, if he does, just try to make sure he keeps his mouth shut and looks pretty."

We were laughing when Ruby came sprinting up out of nowhere and bumped Amber hard as she flew past us.

"Ahh!" Amber stumbled, close to teetering over but quickly regaining her balance.

"Watch out where you're going!" Nila yelled out to deaf ears. I think it was a reflex or a knee-jerk reaction to Ruby hurting Amber rather than a planned rebuttal. The situation had been weighing heavy on Nila since the cafeteria.

Annoyed now, Nila blurted out, "Amber, make sure you give Rusty a big kiss goodnight on Saturday!"

I wasn't sure if Ruby heard Nila but everyone else did. Nobody stopped running but everyone looked at us. Almost everyone. Ruby didn't look back and sprinted further ahead of us.

After the warm-up, Mr. Lavie divided us into teams for indoor soccer. I tried to avoid the ball. I knew I sucked and besides, if I began to show interest, people might start passing me the ball. I didn't want to take that chance. I tried to make it look like I was playing, by running back and forth, following the ball when someone else kicked it. I don't know if Mr. Lavie ever noticed, but he never called me out on it. I was happy with this and my C average in gym class.

Nila is the athletic one of the three of us, and she was on the floor with our nemesis Ruby while Amber and I were benched. Amber lucked out there, I thought. Ruby would have killed her, given the chance. As soft-hearted as Nila is, I was sure she could hold her own with Ruby in a one-on-one fist fight. She was certainly big enough and even strong enough to take her, if need be. Nila is a gentle giant but if Ruby kept pushing her buttons, Nila could do some major damage. I suspected some pent-up aggression inside her was just waiting for the opportunity to come out and say hello.

"What are you wearing Saturday night?" I asked Amber.

She turned toward me to reply, SMUCK!

"Agh!" Amber reached for her head. Ruby had kicked the ball right into the back of her noggin. Amber's eyes welled up with tears and her face turned bright red. Everyone in the class burst out laughing including hot Mr. Lavie. Nila and I turned to Ruby. She stood with a smug look on her face, proud as a peacock at her latest accomplishment.

"Are you okay?" I asked. Amber nodded. I assumed her ego was hurt more than her head. As I looked away, I caught sight of Perry. As if he had seen me, he looked over and directly into my eyes.

CHAPTER 6

After I finished brushing my teeth that night, I crawled into bed. I was tired, but more than that I was stressed out over Amber. I looked up at the lilac walls in my bedroom. They were bare except for the corner with my old wooden school desk. Above it, the walls were covered with posters I'd collected. I didn't mind keeping that one corner busy, but I wanted the rest of my room uncluttered.

Nan told me the color lilac is relaxing and soothing. She said it would be a good choice for my bedroom. She was right. It goes well with the white linoleum floor too. The floor has a pattern of gray squares with colored flowers inside them. Nan gave me the floor. She had the tiles left over from the last time she did hers. That was many years ago.

When she passed, I started using her purple and white duvet. It was almost new then, and the thought of it being hers is still comforting. I keep her rosary beads hanging from the wooden headboard of my bed. They are also purple, only a much darker hue. My Nan was not religious, but she would say that she was spiritual. She kept the rosary beads hanging off the head of her own bed. I think they gave her some sense of security, but I never did ask.

That night, I chose to meditate. I wanted to forget gym class and relax. I started with my deep breathing, and I began to clear my mind.

I got comfortable and inhaled a deep breath. I tried to focus on my third eye and see a speck of light. I breathed deep breaths and tried to clear my mind of all thought, but I felt anxious feeling and it was difficult to reach a meditative state. This used to happen when I first started. I followed Nan's advice to count from one to five, over and over, along with my breaths.

I took in a deep breath, one I thought in conjunction with my breath, another deep breath with two, deep breath three…. My mind started relaxing as I kept going over the numbers in my head, breathing along as I went.

It's an alternative to counting sheep. Nan said that you use enough brain power to keep your mind from wandering, but it can be too relaxing. When it worked too well, I'd end up falling asleep. It happened to me again. I was soon fast asleep.

"Violet… Violet… Violet…" I heard my name again. It was the same voice from my dream the night before. She sounded like she was far away. Her call was soft and faint. I followed the voice. I was walking in total darkness and the air chilled me. As I got closer to her voice, I could start to see my surroundings and it was getting warmer with every step. I continued walking, following her voice along a riverbank.

The river was not the blue-green color I expected. It was water but flowing with the colors from my dream the night before – red, orange, yellow, green, blue, indigo, and violet. The colors flowed in rows like a rainbow, individual but unified at the same time. As I walked the sky grew lighter until it was a brilliant white. I thought I should cover my eyes, but it did not hurt.

The landscape was clearer than I had ever seen. The colors were more vivid and the edges of everything were sharper. It was breathtaking. Plants were tall and lush in every direction. Trees with fruits in all the colors of the rainbow crowded the sides of the river. Everything was larger and more superior, fat fish jumped up high from the river in plenty.

I dove in. As I entered the water, I felt I belonged, like I was one with it. It was warm and inviting. I smelled a sweet perfume of flowers and balsam. The long white night-gown I was wearing did not hinder my swimming, and I was able to breathe under water. I swam with the fish through the colors of the water running red, orange, yellow, green, blue, indigo, and violet. The colors intensified as I swam deeper, but it did not get darker.

The swimming did not tire me – it gave me energy. My strength and my spirit grew with every stroke. I swam until I found a gold treasure chest sitting among the brightly colored smooth stones on the bottom of the riverbed. There was a padlock on the box, but the key was in the lock. I hesitated briefly but chose to open the chest. I turned the key, removed the lock, and lifted the lid.

The treasure chest was not filled with gold or diamonds. It was almost empty, with a scroll of white paper at the bottom. I picked it up and stretched it out. It stayed floating in front of me, unrolled. I read the dark gold lettering:

THE KEY TO THE COLORS

FROM THE BOOK OF BEING

RED – PHYSICAL, STRONG, ADVENTURER,
REALIST

ORANGE – PHYSICAL, DAREDEVIL,
THRILL-SEEKER, RISK-TAKER

YELLOW – EMOTIONAL, FUN-LOVING,
CHILDLIKE, JOYFUL

GREEN – MENTAL, INTELLECTUAL,
POWERFUL, HEALER

BLUE – EMOTIONAL, NURTURING,
SENSITIVE, CARETAKER

INDIGO – SPIRITUAL, FORERUNNER,
PSYCHIC, FUTURE

VIOLET – SPIRITUAL, LEADERS,
TEACHERS, VISIONARIES

The scroll disintegrated and washed away when I read the last words. I started to rise to the surface of the water and woke up. I grabbed a sheet of paper from my desk and wrote the passage down as fast as I could. I tried not to forget anything. I studied that piece of paper many times over, in the months that followed.

CHAPTER 7

The next day was different. I was different.

My alarm went off at seven. It was Friday morning. I woke up and did a few yoga stretches along to a video Mom picked up for me at the library called "Morning Stretch." It was a beginner's tape, so it was quick and easy. After stretching, I flow better, and it lasts throughout the day. My muscles start to tense after I miss a day or two.

I got dressed and went to the bathroom to get washed up. I looked in the mirror and something was different. There was something there I hadn't seen before. I could see the color purple surrounding me. I wasn't sure if it was me, or the mirror. "What the?" I wiped the mirror and rubbed my eyes, but nothing changed. I tried squinting and moving closer to the mirror, but it was still there. I wasn't sure what to think. I shook my head and went downstairs for breakfast.

The house was empty. Friday mornings my mom and dad took Mara to "Baby's First Books" at the library. They make a day out of it. We don't have much money, so this was their way of treating themselves every week. The three of them would go out for breakfast beforehand, and then run a few errands after. I did not mind being left out, I enjoyed the break. And besides, Mom would pick up a few videotapes for me from the library to watch over the weekend. It was win for everyone.

I decided to scramble up a couple of eggs. I ate them with toast and butter along with a glass of milk. I like making breakfast for myself on Fridays. I love to cook, the few things I can, and it doesn't take long. It's the way I liked to treat myself on Fridays too. After I finished eating, I left for school.

Nila was walking toward the path between our houses. It was early March, so the grass was still brown, and the trees were still bare. The sun was out, but everything looked gray. It is such a stark contrast to my dream from last night, I thought. That place was divine, like being on another planet.

As we approached one another I saw something around Nila, something I hadn't seen before. There was a gleam of blue light that caught my eye. It was peeking out from above her right shoulder.

"Hi Nila." I said. "Are you feeling okay today?" I was startled by the light, and I wanted to be sure Nila hadn't grown a spotlight or somehow was super charged last night. I suspected the only difference in Nila was how I saw her.

"I feel great," Nila replied. "Do I look pale? I'm trying a BB cream today and I hate having anything on my face. I wasn't sure if I should wear it today."

"Oh shoot! Sorry, no, you look great," I said hoping not to draw any more attention to the subject. "Mom told me there was a cold going around so I thought I would just check in on you. That's all, nothing serious. Don't want my bestie coming down with something right before March Break." I decided to fib, for now anyways, since maybe my eyes *were* playing tricks on me. Hopefully, it's not glaucoma, I thought.

We walked together in the sun, enjoying the mild weather and each other's company. The privileged kids from Glencarter Junior High get a drive to school every day. Nila and I were not those kids. We walked most mornings regardless of the weather.

Getting a ride was not an option. Mom's never had a driver's license and Dad says he doesn't like to waste gas driving the car to save a ten-minute walk. When it rains or snows, Dad says "You aren't sugar Violet. You two won't melt." It has to be downright horrendous, like Hurricane Juan weather, for Dad to drive us. Elizabeth, Nila's mom, doesn't own a car. I don't remember her ever having one. Nila has a larger extended family than I do and there is always a relative willing to cart her mom around, but not to give us a ride to school.

As we walked, we talked, mostly about Amber's big date tomorrow. I watched Nila as we went. "Only one more sleep until Amber's date with Rusty. I'm not sure who's more excited, me or Amber?" Nila laughed.

When Nila got excited for Amber the gleam of blue light started extending out around her. It looked like it was coming from her entire body. I could see a shimmer in the light that moved with Nila. It flowed along with her almost like waves in the ocean. The blue light continued to grow until it became a bright blue sparkly haze that completely engulfed her.

"I'm happy for her too, but then there's Ruby." I rolled my eyes.

"I swear, I'm going to say something if Ruby makes Amber cry again today." When Nila began talking about Ruby the blue haze began to diminish. It withdrew into her body as she spoke.

Nila is my best friend, and I wanted to tell her something was going on, but this was too strange. I opted to continue keeping this to myself. As we walked down the corridors, everyone I saw had hazes of color around them. Since people were standing close, their auras overlapped, but the colors didn't blend in those areas creating new ones. Everyone's auras were the same colors as my dreams. Some were large and sparkling, dazzling to the eye. Others seemed small, hugging their bodies tight, hardly even noticeable. The brightness and shades varied too. I wondered if I had actually woken up. Could I still be dreaming?

I was so taken by the colors surrounding everyone that I didn't notice Amber's absence from the bench where we normally meet her at the entryway. Hell, I didn't even notice the bench that morning. I walked straight to Mrs. Walker's class with Nila like I was in a trance, or under some spell.

"Amber isn't at her seat either, Vi," Nila announced, breaking my train of thought, and bringing me back to reality.

"That's odd," I said, "maybe she's out of town." I had no idea where Amber was.

"Or maybe she's with Rusty. He could have met up with her and decided to walk her to class." Nila guessed.

That wasn't the case though. Amber wasn't with Rusty. He arrived a few minutes later, in a cloud of orange that rushed through the classroom door with Alex and Craig. Nila and I looked at each other, concerned, but more confused. Amber was a no show at school all day. Was this her way of getting out of the date? After the week Amber had she was due for a little fun.

The rest of the school day, I studied auras. During Geometry when Jeremy answered an equilateral triangle instead of an isosceles triangle, I noticed that his aura shrank in size and hugged his skin. I could tell he was embarrassed. I saw this sort of reaction throughout the day when someone got a question wrong.

The opposite happened when they were correct. Their auras would expand and get sparkly, like when Suzy got the formula correct in Sodium Hydroxide in Chemistry class, NaOH. Her aura grew so large, it almost engulfed three kids. I could not wait to get home that night to see what colors my family members were.

I discovered that Dad was strong red, Mom was a thoughtful green, Mara was a pale yellow, and I was still violet. We were a colorful household.

Nila was spending the night at my house. We had planned it a week earlier, but I was regretting it when the evening came. It didn't have anything to do Nila. I love spending time with her, probably more than anyone else. That night, though, I wanted to do research on the lights I saw emanating from everyone. I consoled myself with the idea of studying Nila instead.

I was both confused and relieved Nila still had the blue light around her when she showed up at my house. As soon as she arrived, she wanted to call Amber. "Let's see if the call goes through." I felt bad. I hadn't even thought of Amber since I got home. I was so preoccupied with the colors that my mind had been spinning all day. "I tried calling a couple of times since I got home from school, but there's no answer." Nila said.

We tried again, same thing. "It's frustrating!"

"I hope she's okay. It unusual for her to disappear like this."

"I'm sure she's fine, Nila or we would have heard something by now. Bad news spreads like wildfire in Glencarter."

We went up to my room, to watch movies on a small, older TV that was Nan's. Mom had picked out some good videotapes from the library, since our selection was not the best. We had two bottles of Coke, a box of chocolate covered peanuts, and a large bag of chips. We were set for a night of gossip, munchies, and movies.

The first movie we watched was *Romeo + Juliet*. Nila was very emotional. She went through the ups and downs right along with the main characters, as if she was in the movie. At the end, Nila bawled her eyes out. I never *really* noticed before how much Nila cries. But once I began to think about it, I remembered Nila crying on many occasions. She's cried over births and at weddings, and of course funerals, though that's a given. She cries during any moment or event with strong feelings. I've seen her cry when she was happy, sad, mad, or glad. She has even cried over music videos!

That night I was more aware of how her emotions swelled, taking over and getting the best of her. Through the uplifting times in the movie the light surrounding her grew large, bright, and sparkly. During the sad times it would come close and tight to her body.

I looked over and Nila was asleep soon after we put the second movie on. It was Clueless starring Alicia Silverstone. It was a few years old, and we had watched it many times before. We hadn't seen it for a while, so I thought we would enjoy it, but I couldn't blame her for falling asleep. We can practically recite every word and it had been a long week. Nila's aura receded when she fell asleep, and there were hardly any sparkles visible but the ones I did see rocked back and forth with her breath.

Like most times, I was the yin to Nila's yang. It took me a long time to get to sleep that night. My mind was racing as I lay there. I felt dizzy. Should I wake Nila up, I thought, tell her about my dreams and my day? I wanted to but I was not sure how to explain what I was seeing to Nila. I didn't understand it myself. I let Nila rest.

Where could Amber be? Where could Amber be? My thoughts repeated as I rolled around in my bed, trying not to wake Nila. I hoped Amber was safe. I prayed.

God, thank you for this new gift. I'm not sure why I have it but hopefully you will send the answers soon. PS, please send Amber home safe and sound. It's not like her to disappear. I'm sure she's okay but we are worried.

I repeated this over and over in my head until the words came so slowly, they stopped. I'd fallen asleep. I slept through the night, but I didn't dream.

Nila went home Saturday morning. "Call me as soon as you hear from her!" Nila said before she left.

"Yes, and I'll tell you everything I find out about her date with Rusty, that's if she even ended up going."

"Between the two of us we should get *almost* the entire story from her." Nila winked.

CHAPTER 8

Amber called early Saturday afternoon.

"I'm so happy to hear from you! Where have you been?"

"My parents sprang a last-minute trip, Thursday after school." Amber explained. "It was really rushed. We left that evening to visit my great aunt, Sally. She lives an hour away in St. Andrews. The timing was terrible. I only agreed to go because Mom *promised* we'd be back home Saturday. I wasn't going to miss my date with Rusty. By the time I had my bag packed my parents were ready to go. I meant to call you, but then forgot. I knew I was forgetting something when we left."

"We were so worried about you. We didn't know what happened to you."

"My cousins just came home from working away out west. They were in Calgary. We all spent the night there together. It was so much fun! Our family filled the kitchen, with a feast of food and drinks, lots of singing and dancing. Remember Uncle Merrill?"

I did. I met him a few times over the years. He's a nice man.

"He played the guitar and others joined in on the spoons, tambourines and there was a boot someone had brought home from Newfoundland. Have you seen one of these before?"

"I can't say that I have." I laughed.

"It's literally a broom handle with bottle caps attached to it and it comes with a stick. You beat it off the floor while banging it with the stick. I tried playing it since it takes no talent but it's heavier than it looks. You really need to have upper body strength and I'm not strong or coordinated, so it didn't work out very well. My family got a good laugh out of watching me attempt it!"

I was relieved. "Nila and I were totally freaking out. We thought something could have happened to you or even worse… that you were backing out of the date." I teased. "I am happy you're okay and that you *are* going." I laughed. "I can't wait to hear all about it"

"It'll probably be too late to call when I get home tonight, but I'll call you as soon as I get up tomorrow and let me know how things go."

"Sounds good. I hope you guys have fun tonight, we'll talk soon." I hung up the phone.

Mom and Dad went to a family friend's house that evening for a game of cards. They play Forty-Fives during the winter months to help pass the time. It can be bleak here. As I said before, there's not much to do here during the winter.

They left about seven o'clock, after they tidied up the supper stuff and cleaned themselves up too. So, I was home alone that Saturday night babysitting Mara. My job was to entertain Mara until she was ready to go to bed. She usually went down around eight or eight-thirty. It could be earlier if she hadn't napped that day.

Mara was on a blanket I had stretched out for her, playing with a handful of toys. She used to enjoy being in her jumper or saucer but now that she was close to crawling, she preferred honing her new skills on the floor. I lay down beside her, flipping through a new *Seventeen* magazine that arrived in the mail this week. Mom had bought me a subscription for my birthday. I liked reading the articles about the celebrities and checking out what they were wearing in the pictures. Sometimes I drew silly faces on the ones I don't like so much. I was hoping to get a cool new poster inside, but this month's copy didn't have one.

As we lay there together, Mara kept grabbing my magazine.

"Stop Mara!" I warned, to no avail. What else can entertain her, I thought, as I looked around our living room. There were a couple of things that Mara was really into, besides Mom. One was the TV show *Blue's Clues* – she loves dogs – and another was music. The faster the tempo, the more she liked it. I remembered that Mom had picked up a CD for Mara at the library. I went into the kitchen and got the CD off the counter. It was *Mother Goose & More* from *Sharon, Lois & Bram*. Mom told me they had listened to it earlier that day and Mara really enjoyed song nineteen, "ABC Jig." I turned it on.

A, B, C, D, E, F, G… The song went through the alphabet. The verses were old nursery rhymes, and the chorus was the alphabet. It's quite catchy. The beat's fast, and it's heavy on the accordion. It sounded like good old Maritime music; the kind Merrill would play at a kitchen party.

Mara sat up on her blanket. She cooed as she rocked back and forth, clapping along to the music. Perfect, I thought, as I picked up my magazine and continued flipping through the pages, pen in hand.

I stopped at an article I saw on dream interpretation. The first dream discussed was being unprepared for a test. I've had that one a few times. It said, it means that you have an important, upcoming life challenge that you fear failing. I started thinking about my dreams with the colors, and the unusual experiences I was having, seeing them around people. In the afternoon I had done some internet research and found out that the hazes of light are called auras. I still didn't know for sure if they were real, if I'd keep seeing them, or if it would stop just as suddenly as it began. What was the meaning? Was there any meaning? Would the puzzle pieces ever fit together?

Mara's pale yellow aura grew outward and sparkled faintly as she rocked back and forth, clapping her hands to the music. We had a family joke about Mara's clapping. She could literally clap her little baby hands as loud as Mom could. We always had a good laugh when she did it. I wrote the word *music* in my magazine and beside it the word *mystic*. The spellings are so similar and both words represent things that make Mara and I feel so happy. Could there be other connections too?

By the time the CD reached song twenty-nine, "Lavender's Blue," the tempo dropped, and Mara's eyelids were doing the same. I prepared a bottle, picked her up, and rocked her in my arms until the CD was over and she was sound asleep. I carried her carefully to her crib in Mom and Dad's room. I gently settled her down into her bed for the night.

Now what, I thought, as I went back downstairs. I took the baby monitor receiver off the top of the fridge and turned it on just in case Mara woke up. I decided to have a quick shower, then get into bed for some TV before sleep. As I walked to the bathroom, baby monitor in hand, I wondered how Amber was getting along on her date with Rusty.

Rusty liked Amber, since he asked her out, and I knew Amber liked him. Who wouldn't? But Amber had to be hurting, from all the drama that was going down between her and Ruby. That was tough. I wondered if it was worth it, since we are only in the ninth grade and it's not like he is the *one* or they'd be married someday. It wasn't completely impossible, but it wasn't realistic to think that way. Not in this day and age, anyway. I assumed it would probably be a fling or a six-month relationship, tops. I just hoped, for Amber's sake, the date was going well, and it would all be worthwhile. Ruby may even back off next week, I thought. After she finds out Amber and Rusty are a couple, if that is the case. The whole Amber, Ruby, Rusty thing was too much to worry about when I was trying to understand auras and my dreams.

I set the baby monitor down beside the sink in the bathroom. I turned the shower water on and undressed. After getting the temperature the way I like it, I eased myself in. The heat penetrated deep into my muscles as the water bounced off my shoulders and back. I began to decompress. I opened the shampoo that Mom got on sale the week before. I squeezed enough into my hands to wash my hair and I was lathering it in when I heard voices coming from outside the shower. It sounded like I was eavesdropping in on a conversation and it was coming from the baby monitor. What in the hell!

The voices were muffled, not strong enough to be coming from the TV in my parent's room where the base of the monitor is set up. It didn't matter, that TV wasn't even turned on. I could not hear what was being said but I could tell it was a girl and a man talking.

Was I picking up a conversation from someone else's cordless phone? I experienced that before. Once, on our cordless, I listened to a call between Nila's mom and Nila's Aunt Debbi. I ended up getting some gossip out of it too. Debbi was crying on the phone; she'd caught her boyfriend at the time, messing around with another women.

It never happened before with the baby monitor though, and overhearing the voices made me uneasy. I rinsed my hair and shut off the water. I strained my ears to see if I could recognize the voices. Waves of static blasted from the monitor before it started to squeal. I heard that before. It happens when people are walking too close to the transmitter. I went from thinking this is weird to being completely freaked out. I started shivering, and it was not just from being cold. I peeked around the shower curtain, saw nothing. I reached for the monitor and turned it off. The room became completely quiet except for water dripping in the shower. I got out and wrapped a towel loosely around myself and ran to my parent's room to check on Mara. She was still sound asleep.

I tip toed out of my parents' room. "Hello?" The house was silent, but I had the feeling that Mara and I were not alone. I hurried to my room and practically jumped into my PJs. I went back to my parent's room and turned on the TV, with the volume low. I wanted the company. I felt more secure having Mara with me, not that she would be able to help me much. I took the phone with me, hoping I wouldn't need to call 911. I waited up for Mom and Dad. Our car pulled into the driveway just past eleven-thirty. I ran to my room, into my bed, and under the covers.

CHAPTER 9

Sunday morning, I yawned when I woke up. I was exhausted from the night before. It was late by the time I got to sleep. My mind raced for most of the night. I tried praying and meditating but neither helped. I worried, even after Mom and Dad arrived home. I could not shake off the feeling that I was being watched.

The phone rang early.

"Hi, Vi!" It was Amber. "Our night was pure utter perfection." She sounded excited. "We went to see an action movie. I really didn't want to see it, but Rusty had heard it was good. It wasn't that bad, but the movie wasn't that important." I pictured Amber sitting on her bed twirling her hair in her fingers, her aura large and bright. "He behaved like a complete gentleman. He seemed interested in the stuff I was saying, and he paid for everything. We split a popcorn and a bag of Smarties, *my* favorite. We did each have our own soda, so it wasn't like he was being cheap, just romantic."

"That was nice of him," I said. "Although a lot of people prefer going Dutch these days, don't want to mislead anyone."

"Right. So, Rusty put his arm around me at the beginning of the movie and he kept it there the *whole* night. He didn't even do the old yawn stretch technique, just a shoot your shot, sort of thing. I liked that. He wasn't too forward, but it seems like he really likes me. After the movie was over, he walked me home."

"I'm happy, if you're happy, Amber and you sound thrilled." I smiled. "You deserve it, especially after all the crap between you and Ruby."

"Before Rusty left, he asked me to go to one of his games to watch him play hockey. He has one coming up next Sunday, the playoffs just started."

Amber's not a puck bunny. She doesn't even like hockey, but she likes Rusty. He might let her wear his hockey jacket soon, I thought, *if* they keep seeing each other.

"I heard that they are playing Tuesday night too, but it's an away game out of town."

"What should I get for him for his birthday?" Amber asked.

Rusty's birthday was coming up, on March twenty-second. It's no secret. I think everyone from our elementary class knows everyone else's birthdays, or at least the month. The joys of living in a small town!

"In Glencarter? It is almost impossible to get him anything good here."

"I know and my parents are not planning a trip to the city."

"If Mom and Dad take me to the city shopping before Rusty's birthday, I will gladly pick up a gift for you to give to him," I promised.

"You're the best! I'm going to call Nila and see if she will too."

I did not see Nila or myself heading into the city before Rusty's birthday, but I admired Amber's initiative.

"So Amber, he never kissed you goodnight?" I could not help but ask.

"Just a little one," she hesitantly replied, "not really even worth mentioning." She giggled before saying goodbye.

Nila called me after she hung up the phone with Amber and we compared stories. "It sounds like she told you the same thing, she told me," Nila said, "except Amber left one thing out. I almost died when she said that Rusty was a great kisser and he had very *soft lips*."

We laughed.

Amber didn't tell me what a great kisser Rusty was or how soft his lips are. She may have been thinking it's something I wouldn't do, and I'd judge her on it. I would never do that, but Amber was getting a reputation. She dated a couple of guys from senior high school. Nothing seemed to stick, but people in high school definitely kiss, they definitely make out, and some go even further than that.

Amber developed faster than anyone else in our class. That, along with her good looks and lack of parental supervision may not have been the best combination. She gets loads of attention and not just from the boys. I heard a lot of girls in high school don't like her.

At first, I decided the older girls were jealous of Amber, or even intimidated. She is beautiful and fun to be around, and the older girls wouldn't like the attention she got from the boys. Then I realized Amber never went into details with me and Nila about any of her dates. At least not the interesting parts, the stuff we really wanted to know. I guess deep down I am as nosy as everyone else in Glencarter, but her reluctance made me suspect the rumors could have some truth to them. I can't tell you if Amber flirted with anyone's boyfriend or if the older guys were trying to take advantage of her, but I thought there might be more to it than she was saying. Her silence spoke volumes.

I was sure Ruby believed that Rusty was only interested in Amber because he could probably shake the sheets at The Sugar Shack with her. All that aside, she really was tough competition when it came to Rusty. Amber isn't just beautiful, she is very charismatic and it's hard to put it into words but there is something about her, a spark that pulls people in. She's a free spirit but driven and smart, even though she could be quite naive.

Rusty liked Amber and their date sounded wonderful. I could not blame Ruby for being jealous. There was a little, teeny, tiny part of me that was jealous of her too.

Ruby already knew most of the popular girls in high school through her brothers. I'd hate for them to gang up on Amber next year. She's already been having a rough go and who knows, maybe Ruby isn't that innocent. She might throw herself all over Rusty, if she could do it and save face about town. That would hurt Amber too.

Sundays at my place are quiet. I would have invited Nila over for a while, if I wasn't so tired. I lazed around the house, mostly stretched out across my favorite chair in the living room watching TV, or pretending to watch TV, while I studied Mara and my parent's auras. Dad's red aura was large and bright, as was Mom's green one. The same colors as Ruby and Beryl, I noted. That color combination must be suited for one another.

"I'm really tired. I think I'm just going to go to bed early" I said to Mom and Dad, deciding to turn in for the night.

I wonder what Ruby's reaction will be tomorrow at school, I thought as I got into bed. I was almost certain Ruby was in her own bed, wondering how Amber and Rusty's date went.

I'm going to say a prayer for Amber and for a good outcome. It can't hurt.

God almighty, I've heard of unanswered prayers. I know you will do what is best for everyone involved. But, if possible, please have Rusty ask Amber to be his girlfriend. Amen.

Soon after I finished praying, I felt myself slipping away into sleep. I couldn't keep my eyes open. Understandably so, since I was exhausted.

I was walking through a long tunnel. It was like a train tunnel in an old movie, but instead of being surrounded by dark, I was surrounded by light. The tunnel was filled with rows of lights. The light lined the road and rose over my head in colored rows. It looked like a long rainbow. I knew the light was full of love. The lights were all the colors I was seeing around people – red, orange, yellow, green, blue, indigo, and violet.

As I walked, I felt as if the light and I were becoming one. The light permeated through my skin. Pins and needles of joy were coursing through my entire being. I heard the same voice calling my name again. "Violet... Violet... Violet..." I followed it to a large stone doorway at the end of the tunnel.

The door looked cold and creepy, like something I'd see at Perry's house, I assumed. I opened the door and walked into a large room. The room was warm and white. There was a white circular stone table, in the center of the room. Seven empty seats circle around it. I sat down in the chair closest to the door.

"Violet."

I turned to see a young female figure standing in a dark corner of the room. She came toward me and into the light. She had dark hair and eyes, like me. She was about my age and she was short. We resembled one another. We even had the same color auras. There was one exception, this girl had the most immense and brilliant aura. Her light was more than a haze. Purple beamed out from all around her tiny frame with what looked like millions of stars moving in the sky. She was cosmic!

"Hello Violet," she began. "It is nice to finally meet you. Please call me Seven." As she spoke, violet sparks ignited from the light surrounding her. It was the most beautiful and magical thing I'd ever seen. It reminded me of the Canada Day fireworks but a thousand times better. "You must have many questions about the changes you've been experiencing. I'm here to answer some of these questions for you Violet. The lights you see emanating from people are called *auras*."

I had found this term online when I started seeing them. Now I had confirmation of what it was. I looked at her, wanting to hear more.

"All beings carry and emit energy. The average person, while at rest, generates a hundred watts of power. You would expect people to glow like light bulbs." Her aura lit up for a moment, and she continued. "However, today, most cannot see this energy even though it is possible and not through your third eye." Seven's third eye appeared in the center of her forehead and blinked before it disappeared again, "but with the naked eye."

"An individual's aura reflects one's true self. It is like a window into their soul, revealing their inner truth." It was hard for me to concentrate as I watched what looked like diamonds ebb and flow around Seven. I was completely entranced by the beauty of her spirit.

"Violet," Seven said, "everyone in your dimension or realm, if you will, is capable of seeing auras. But most people have lost their spiritual connection with themselves and with the universe.

"I want you to think back. I am going to tell you about the Mayans." I wasn't sure that I heard of them before but as she finished that sentence, I was staring at a series of pictures that appeared in front of me. I saw pictures of shamans, stone tools, graffiti drawings overlapping each other, the number zero, and more. "They were a wise and ancient civilization. The Mayans constructed calendars based on astrology and the last date recorded is December 21, 2012.

"Some theorists predicted that this date is doomsday or the end of time. And in some respects that is true. But the date is not marking an end to time itself, but an end of time as we know it. It marks the beginning of a new time, and we are now in a transition period. Over the next forty years an era will end, the technical, and a new one will begin, the spiritual age.

"It's a spiritual awakening or enlightenment for humanity. This new era is progressive and positive. It's part of our evolution." The slide show ended with images of three calendars. I turned and our eyes locked. We connected with one another.

"The scroll you found in the treasure chest is an excerpt from a chapter of *The Book of Being*. It serves as a guide, passed on to us from our ancients." As she talked, the scroll appeared from the sparkles in her aura. It unwrapped and a rainbow-colored light shot out from it. "The passage revealed to you is called 'The

Key to the Colors.' It explains how an individual's personality traits are predetermined, just like your eye color, from the moment of conception."

"Every soul's main personality traits correspond to their prominent aura color. For the scroll to be most beneficial, please review the secrets within it and apply the knowledge to the people you know and to your surroundings."

"If a person's aura is large and bright, the person is happy, and their energy is stable with the energy around them. They are positive." Her aura brightened and grew out. "If a person's aura is small and murky, the person is unhappy, and their energy is unstable with their environment. In that moment, their forces are negative." Her aura withdrew into her body, before returning to its splendid size and breathtaking display.

"Someone might have a small aura if they are feeling insignificant over something or someone. Another reason is they could be telling a lie or physically ill. You will be able to read people better and recognize the signs, after you've had some time to develop your new gifts."

"Violet, I must mention more manifestations to you. A few colors are connected to certain emotions an individual is feeling at a specific time. These colors are true tells or glimpses into the person's state of mind. They will show up as sparks or bursts of color in an aura when the feelings arise."

"Red shows anger, blue represents love, and green is envy." Red, blue, and green sparks ignited out from her violet aura. "I have one more sign to tell you about before our lesson is complete for the night, perhaps one of the most important for you to understand. There is something else that can affect an aura, another factor. It is called a red overlay."

What is a red overlay? I didn't read about that term online, I thought.

"It is a red outer shell surrounding an aura, a shield that protects a person from the outside world." A red band appeared around the outside of Seven's aura. "An overlay appears from trauma at a young age. This is someone who has suffered abuse, abandonment, or neglect. The protective barrier was created as an act of self-defense, to avoid future emotional trauma."

I couldn't think of anyone I knew, who would have a red overlay.

"A person will use it until they feel safe, and it is no longer necessary. At this time, they will shed the red overlay and their spirit will finally be free." The band around Seven burned bright before it exploded, the remnants turned to ash and fell to the floor, grass appeared to sprout before it disappeared.

"Violet, I know this is a lot to learn, especially all at once, but you have received a glorious gift. Do not be overwhelmed or afraid. You will always be protected by us, your guardian angels, and by your Nan." Seven of the sparkles inside of my aura grew larger, like stars that twinkled white light. "We are always with you, even when we don't reveal ourselves to you."

"You will start noticing things you didn't see or hear before. It is all good, rest assured of that. You were just not as woke or aware as you have become. You will start seeing more coincidences in your everyday life, events that will steer you in certain directions. They've always been there but are more prominent now."

The room was fading, as Seven was finishing. "Our lesson is done for tonight. It has been my pleasure getting to know you better. My mentor will be introducing himself to you soon. I've been working with him for a long time."

Seven was gone and the room became my room. I was awake. Confused, I shook my head until it started to clear. It was Monday morning, and the sun was up. To cut costs, my parents turn the heat down at our house for the night. The temperature was cold, but I was drenched in sweat. I grabbed the wired notebook, I started keeping in my nightstand. I wrote down everything that I remembered.

CHAPTER 10

Nila and I met on the path between our houses for the walk to school. Nila's aura was bright and large.

"Nila, you look like you're in a great mood this morning. You are radiating!"

Nila's aura grew even bigger and her cheeks blushed. "Thank you so much! I don't think anyone has ever told me that before but yes, I'm happy Amber's date went well. I was worried about her last week."

She really appreciated the compliment and Nila was genuinely happy for Amber. I could see it as white and blue sparks ignited and shifted in her aura. Nila's huge heart is why people who know her love her so much. She is a true blue and she returns love tenfold.

Amber was at the bench inside the entrance, waiting for us to arrive. Since Amber was absent from school Friday, this was the first time I saw her aura.

Yellow! I knew it! I thought, as we approached Amber. She looked like a ball of sunshine, except for one thing. It couldn't be! The closer we came to her the more pronounced it became. This was something I never expected, I was shocked. Amber had a deep red overlay, hugging her otherwise perfect yellow aura.

What in the hell... I had trouble grasping it. We were best friends forever and I could not recall anything abusive or traumatic ever happening to her. If anything, I always thought the opposite of Amber. She was the girl who seemed to have it all. She is smart, pretty, has a nice house, and that body! Ruby had been making her life miserable, but only recently, and I was certain it would only be temporary.

"Good morning." Nila greeted Amber as we met her.

"Hi, Amber," I mustered, as we walked away from the main doors.

"I'm back!" Amber sang. "So, guess who called me last night?" Amber did not wait for us to answer. "Rusty, and we talked for over an hour. He gives good phone," I looked at Nila trying not to laugh, "and we actually have quite a few things in common." Amber giggled "This could be the beginning of a real relationship. But I don't want to jinx it. We *know* I haven't really had much luck with relationships, but I think that's about to change."

"No doubt about it," Nila said. I nodded in agreement as we took our seats in Mrs. Walker's English class. I normally would have rolled my eyes at that last remark from Amber, but I could not stop thinking about Amber's red overlay. I had trouble focusing on anything else. My eyes turned to the doorway as Rusty and his friends pushed their way in.

"Am I the only one that didn't get my homework done?" Alex asked. His voice boomed above the classroom clatter. They were loud and disruptive, as usual. Following closely behind was Ruby with her trusty sidekick Beryl.

The second bell rang, and Mrs. Walker started roll call.

"Alex,"

"Here!"

"Beryl,"

"Present."

I knew our teacher was married, with no children, but for the first time I sensed sadness over that, and her students helped to compensate. Her blue aura was dim and close to her body. Some areas were murky, and I didn't see any sparkles in it.

The kids in junior high are not always on their best behavior, and this morning's roll call was no exception. Everyone kept talking as she made her way through it. Mrs. Walker tolerated that behavior from us, more than any of our other teachers did.

"Hi Amber." Rusty looked over at her as he sunk down into his seat.

"Good morning, Rusty," Amber replied. Her cheeks turned a pale pink. Her yellow aura brightened and grew out around her. Her red overlay became bigger too.

"Hi Rusty," said Ruby, as she rushed past for her desk. "Great game the other night. You guys are playing awesome this season!"

"Hey Ruby." Rusty's aura grew brighter when he spoke to Ruby. "Thanks, we are trying."

Rusty turned his attention back to Amber. "What's going on this week? Do you have anything planned?"

I was a taken aback. Rusty's aura grew when he talked with Amber, but not near as much as it did with Ruby.

Ruby vied for Rusty's attention. "How was your weekend, Rusty? What did you do?"

"It was great, thanks Ruby," Rusty returned, ignoring her second question. "How did your football game go?"

"It was good. You know it's always a good time when my brothers get together."

As Rusty and Ruby talked back and forth, I could not believe what I saw. Rusty's aura grew bigger and brighter as he talked with Ruby. His orange aura looked dazzling as Ms. Walker continued with the class roll call. His aura did grow and glitter for Amber, but it was insignificant compared to the changes during his interactions with Ruby. I didn't know what this meant. Perhaps nothing. Rusty was talking about stuff he gets excited about with Ruby, sports and himself.

I wish I had someone to discuss this with, I thought.

"Class, we are at the end, this is the last name. If you haven't caught up on the weekend news by now, it will have to wait until after class. Perry Van Winkle?"

"P-present," Perry stammered.

I looked at Perry, and our eyes locked. Could it be? Is Perry the answer to my prayers? He *is* an Indigo. I could clearly see that. Indigos are psychic and forerunners for what the future will bring. Knowing this, explained a lot about Perry and his peculiar nature.

I sensed Perry was familiar with auras and I knew he had gifts of his own. I pondered the idea. Seven *did* say events will steer me in certain directions! I am going to send him an email during computer class.

CHAPTER 11

I looked at the clock. Computer class was almost over. I had butterflies in my stomach. I was nervous but I felt an inner push to send an email to Perry. I don't remember him having any friends, I thought. I hope he doesn't mind me reaching out. I really need a confidant though — someone to reveal my new secrets to. I don't think Nila or Amber will get it, but Perry seems like he might understand this kind of stuff.

I wrote the email. "Hi Perry, I have something I need to ask you about. Can we meet sometime after school? If you don't want to, I completely understand. And no rush, it's nothing serious." The last line was a fib, but I didn't want Perry to think it was an emergency or something bad. I read the message three times to make sure it sounded okay before I hit send.

Seconds later, Perry's face lit up and his aura brightened as it grew. I knew right away my email was well received. I watched him read it and then he started to type. He did not look my way. I stopped when I heard the notification indicating I had a new message. I nervously opened his response.

Perry replied, "Let's meet at my house today at four, my parents work until five."

"Perfect!" I typed back.

I spent the rest of the class sneaking online, trying to find information on auras.

After last class, I was putting books in my locker when Nila walked over ready to head home with me.

"Shoot, sorry Nila, I have homework due tomorrow that I have to stay after school to do research on."

"Do you want me to stay too? Maybe I can help you?"

"That's nice of you to offer but no thanks, Nila, not today." I could feel my aura shrinking. I hated lying to Nila, but I was not ready to reveal my new truth to her. I felt guilty lying but I don't think she minded walking home alone, her aura didn't change.

I called my parents from the pay phone in the corridor by the offices. I gave them same excuse.

"No problem. I'm cooking tuna casserole for supper tonight."

"Yum! One of my faves! Thanks Mom, I won't be late."

Afterwards, I went to the school library. It was only three-fifteen, I had time to kill before going to Perry's. The room smelled of stale paper. I sat down at one of the computer terminals and searched for books on auras. Zero results. That wasn't surprising considering we are in Glencarter, but I think it is worth checking the town library soon, I decided.

I flipped through some *Tiger Beat* magazines for half an hour, then left for Perry's house. I didn't need Perry to tell me where he lived. Glencarter being the small town that it is, I knew it was 51 High Street. I know where almost everyone else in our class lives. Nothing is too far away, and everyone is close.

Perry's house is about a five-minute walk from school, in the opposite direction from my house, and up a hill. Although it's the better side of town, it isn't called the upper end or the upper side or anything pretentious like that. It doesn't have a nickname, like the lower end does.

As I walked up the steep hill which led to Perry's street, I understood how High Street got its name. I was relieved to finally turn onto it.

He lives in a grand old-style home with wooden shingles painted an inviting pale green. The trim is a dark green, with a picket fence that matches, marking the perimeter of the yard. The building is old, but it and the property are well maintained. Both of Perry's parents have good jobs, so they can afford the upkeep. His mother is nurse at a hospital in a larger town not far from here and his father is a police officer in Glencarter.

One of his parents must have a green aura, I thought. You don't often see this much green on a huge house. There were a couple of large trees in the yard and that afternoon a tire slowly swung from one of them, back and forth. I heard a young girl playing and laughing but I couldn't see her.

I got goosebumps as I walked the path leading to the door. My heart was racing and my palms were sweating as I approached it. I looked for a doorbell but there wasn't one. Instead, I found an old metal door knocker. The kind you lift up and hammer down on the door.

Figures, I thought. This is something I expected to see at Perry's place. It is his style, peculiar and a little creepy. I was chuckling to myself as I pounded the knocker down on the door. I hope he heard me and didn't mind the intrusion. I barely finished knocking when he answered the door.

"Hello Violet," Perry said. "Please come in." He gestured his hand for me to walk inside.

"Thank you so much for having me. I hope you don't mind me reaching out." I hesitated, then stepped over the threshold.

"Let's go to the sitting room," he said. "This way."

I followed him, taking a good look around.

The inside of Perry's home was large, open, and old. The furniture looked like costly antiques. I watch Antiques Roadshow on TV with my dad. The people from that show would be in heaven here. The temperature inside the house was unusually cool, even for this time of year. It must be hard to heat, given the size, I thought.

In contrast to the exterior of the house, the inside felt dark. The walls were off-white, and light enough. But there wasn't enough windows and natural light coming in for the space. Almost as a substitute, colorful framed paintings of flowers and birds lined the walls. I shifted my head back and forth admiring them as we went.

"My mother paints." Perry explained, as if he had eyes in the back of his head.

"They are beautiful."

We walked down a couple of hallways. The hardwood floor creaked beneath our feet until we reached his sitting room, at the back of the house. This room was brighter, with lots of windows, like a sun porch. My house doesn't have a sitting room, or a sun porch. Perry motioned to a set of cushioned chairs. He waited for me to sit down before he did.

"Violet, I was surprised that you wanted to meet with me. What is this about?" He looked at me, his eyes narrowed. He didn't waste any time getting to the point. I liked it.

I wish I could say I played it cool and casual, exposing a little to see his reaction. But all it took was this single question from Perry, and I spilled my guts. I started with my first dream about the colors and told him everything. I barely stopped to breathe between sentences.

I studied Perry as I spoke. I tried to tell by his face whether he believed me or not, but I couldn't read him. He didn't react or interrupt, and his aura did not change. He stayed silent when I finished. I assumed he was overwhelmed and processing all the information I just gave him. It was a lot.

"Perry, I see your aura and I know you are an Indigo. Are you familiar with the term and what the color means?" During computer class, I found websites about Indigo children. They sounded like Perry, tending to be social loners, with psychic abilities. That last part intrigued me. I believed Perry would know about them, considering he's one.

"Yes, I am," Perry replied. "Violet, I know what auras and indigos are. I can see them, but I don't interpret auras. I don't like to draw attention to myself, so I try not to look at people for too long." He turned toward one of the windows.

"I have always known you are truly a Violet, Violet." He laughed a little and I saw his aura shift. The indigo mass around him gleamed with glitter, like the sun reflecting off the ocean. The glitter had masses within his aura too. These masses moved within his indigo aura from side to side, then up and down.

"The thing is, Violet, I have some news for you, too." I looked deep in his eyes. "I wasn't *that* surprised when you messaged me. I've been dreaming a Violet was coming to see me. I had no idea who, or why. I've been dreaming about it for three months. I should have realized it would be you, the violet-colored Violet."

Perry paused, as if he was not sure he should tell me something. "I have other gifts, besides seeing auras. I know we're not really friends yet," Perry's aura shifted more, "but I want you to know you can talk to me. Don't be embarrassed. You wouldn't believe half of what I could tell you. I will help you if I can."

As Perry spoke, I felt dizzy, like I was getting lost in his eyes. I found a truth there I hadn't seen before. He was absolute and his eyes corresponded to that. He blinked his eyes and looked away from me, back into the hall.

"Just think about it for now. That's probably enough for one day." He stood and moved toward the door. I followed him.

Perry stands about six-foot tall and is lanky with dark features. He has black hair and olive skin. His eyes are a green that almost glow gold if you look long enough. How hadn't I noticed them before? I suppose, I hadn't really noticed Perry before. Now, I had to look away from him before I was completely drawn in.

Perry's words were just what I needed. I wanted to hear more, but not right then. I hoped it wasn't because my head was dizzy, but it was in this moment I realized that maybe he was not that peculiar and creepy after all. I knew we had more in common and a better connection than I would have ever imagined possible.

"Thank you for having me!" I said, as we walked back down the long corridors. Then, I heard the girl laughing again, the one from outside. I still could not see her.

"Who is that, Perry?" I asked, turning myself around, trying to find her. "Where is she?"

"That's my sister, Maxine." He shrugged. "She likes to hide."

"You have a sister?" I asked Perry. How could he have a sister without me knowing?

"My mom had a miscarriage a few years ago. No one else has ever heard her before."

I was shocked. "I'm so sorry, Perry. I didn't know."

He smiled at me as we reached the door. "I know. I'll see you at school tomorrow."

"Bye for now," I said, as I walked out,

"Goodbye, Violet." Maxine called after me.

"See you later, Maxine."

CHAPTER 12

Tuesday evening, after supper, I walked to the town library.

"Brr," I said to myself, as I pulled the front of my jacket up over my chin and my toque as far down past my ears as possible.

Glencarter had been abnormally warm that winter but the odd night in March, the night temperature still dropped to well below freezing. The humid ocean air is damp and heavy. It's notorious for sinking through your skin. I was cold to the bone.

Not much happened at school that day except for one thing.

"I'm going to the city shopping!" Nila exclaimed when I saw her that morning. Her aura was bright and dazzled in the sun.

"What! When?" I asked, my excitement grew for Amber. "Amber is going to be ecstatic."

"Tomorrow, with my Aunt Debbi!"

Nila couldn't wait to tell Amber. She rushed to school, grinning all the way.

Amber was sitting, waiting for us at the bench.

"Guess who's going to the city shopping tomorrow?" Nila squealed.

"Oh my God, you are?" Amber jumped up from the bench and gave Nila a big hug.

"Yes! You remember my Aunt Debbi? She's pregnant now and she asked if I want to go to the city with her tomorrow for a doctor's appointment and some *shopping*." Nila squealed. "Her boyfriend has to work, and she doesn't want to go alone. She's going to pick me up here, just before lunch."

"I can't believe the timing. That is awesome!" Amber beamed. "So, you don't mind picking me up a birthday gift for Rusty, do you?"

"Of course not, that's what friends are for!"

"Thank you, Nila! I owe you *big* time, for the rest of my life! I'll bring you the money tomorrow morning… I'm thinking cologne."

I was happy for Amber but even happier for Nila. I hadn't been to the city in forever. I knew her and Debbi would go to McDonalds to eat after they were done shopping. It is the only fast food I've ever had besides KFC, who used to have a restaurant in Glencarter before it went out of business back when I was a small kid.

By the time I reached the Town Hall, where the library is, my eyes were watering from the cold and my teeth were chattering. I opened the door and hot air blasted me. That's the warmth you only get from a government building in the winter, I thought. Thank you, God, I needed that. I found my way to an empty computer terminal.

I sat down to search for books on auras. I typed the word into the system and hit find. The results were three books: *What Color is your Aura*, *Life Colors* and *Aura's: How to See, Sense and Know Human Aura Colors*. Wow, maybe Glencarter isn't so far behind the times after all. I scanned the aisles until I found the books. I guess I know how I'd be spending my March Break.

I went to the desk set up in the middle of the large room to check out the three books. An older lady with short white hair and dark blue rimmed glasses greeted me.

"Good evening, young lady? Is it cold enough outside for you?" She laughed, and a soft blue aura sparkled as she smiled. Her voice was rough, and she had deep lines around her eyes and mouth. Our hands touched briefly as I passed her the books. Her hands were very soft to the touch. Like her heart, I thought, like my Nan's.

I started seeing images of her life flash in my mind. In the first one she was a baby being born at the hospital. Her parents were so happy to have her. The pics proceeded through her school years to her high school graduation. She looked so cute in her cap and gown. She was dressed in the Glencarter school colors, maroon and yellow. Next was her wedding day, she made a beautiful bride dressed in white and her husband was dapper as he waited while she walked down the aisle. Then their first home – I immediately recognized the house. It was the one on the corner, with the old bag that yells out the window at us on our way to school. Could she be?

Our hands met once more, after she scanned the books and passed them back to me. When we touched a second time, the visions continued. She was watching her kids in the yard. She had a little boy and a baby girl around Mara's age. Later, she taught them how to garden. Her family had barbeques and played croquet during the summers. They had an outdoor skating rink and snow forts there in winter. The kids continued to grow until they moved away for school. Then her husband died, and the yard was empty. The last vision I saw was her yelling at Nila and me out her kitchen window. A sense of loneliness swept over me and settled into the pit of my stomach.

"It sure is cold enough out tonight. How is your evening going?" I decided to make small talk. I knew she didn't recognize me, and I didn't introduce myself.

"It's going well, dear," she replied. "It's been slow though. The weather must be keeping everyone inside tonight. I only volunteer here one evening a week. It's nice to get out and see people."

"We've been lucky to have had such a mild winter, despite the cold nights."

Her aura brightened. "These books are due back three weeks from today. I'm sure I'll see you again soon."

"Certainly!" I said, knowing there was a good chance she might see me tomorrow morning on my way to school. But we won't walk on her lawn anymore, now that I know what it means to her. "Thank you for the books and I appreciate your time."

I left for home. The cold air was waiting for me when I walked back outside. The wind was facing me on my way home. I went as fast as my legs could carry me.

The library is on Main Street, no more than a fifteen-minute walk from my house on a good day. As I walked past the gas station beside it, a streetlight blew out as I trekked past.

Strange timing, I thought, increasing my pace. Another blew out in the next block, as I walked under it. My heart began to race. I moved even faster to a jog. My breathing got heavy, and my lungs started to burn. Then another light died. I started to run. By the time I reached home, I was sweating. I counted seven streetlights that had blown out along my way.

I was never so happy to be home. I was relieved to be out of the cold, but I was even happier to be safe inside of my house with my family. I wasn't used to seeing anything supernatural, and I was freaking out. Seven streetlights in fifteen minutes! There was no way that was coincidence.

Seven? She did say I would see signs, could that have been her? It was Seven streetlights. Maybe she didn't want me to feel alone, or it was a sign from her that I'm on the right path. It was encouraging and daunting at the same time.

I hung up my coat, put away my boots, and paused outside the living room. Mom and Dad were sitting on the couch watching *Jeopardy*. Mara was playing with toys on a blanket on the floor in front of them.

"I made it back, I'm home," I said.

"Oh, I'm glad, I was worried. It's so cold out tonight." Mom said.

"She was getting ready to send out the troops." Dad pointed his finger toward his face. "That's me, so I'm really glad your home. I almost had to go out in that too."

We laughed, even Mara, she mirrored us.

"I am going up to my room now to study." I ran upstairs, clutching the books tight.

"Going to the library and studying on the same school night. I think this is a first for you. You're so studious all of a sudden." Mom complimented me on my new-found work ethic as I disappeared into my room.

I read through the books late into the night. It was long after midnight when I turned the light off for sleep. I lay still in my bed. I thought back to how I'd felt *special* when I was little. I never knew why, there was no reason for it. Maybe everyone does, or maybe I was compensating for my meager beginnings in the lower end of Glencarter. I'd gotten resigned to nothing changing. Over time I lost that feeling, and I stopped believing it. Then the dreams came, I started seeing auras, and everything started to change, for me and everyone. I was part of it. Maybe there *really* was something to that feeling I had.

I said a prayer before going to sleep.

God, I am grateful for everything in my life – past, present, and future. I pray for your guidance, bring forth people who can lead and influence me in the right ways. I am at your mercy, please protect me. Amen

I was starting to drift off to sleep when I heard faint voices. I wasn't sure if I was awake or dreaming. It sounded like a group chanting a mantra, but I could not make sense of the words. I knew I was being given a message. One of knowledge and power, from the other side, that would reveal itself in due time.

CHAPTER 13

Wednesday morning, Amber was anxious for us to arrive. She met us at the front steps of the school. She couldn't wait to give Nila the money.

"Here you go Nila, fifty dollars." Amber handed Nila the cash. "Hopefully that's enough. Try and find something *really* good on sale, maybe some cologne."

"Sure, no problem," Nila said cheerfully, as she took the money. "I'll do my best." Her aura was the largest I had ever seen it before. It was spectacular. She was delighted to help.

"I'm know you will! I still can't believe you are going today. What luck? Like, it's fate, isn't it? I must be destiny's child."

We laughed.

"You're such a goof!" I said to Amber.

"I almost forgot," Amber turned from me to Nila, "My parents are going to a friend's Friday night, and I was wondering if you two want to come over and hang out? I hate being home alone."

"Sorry Amber," Nila replied. "I can't. I promised Aunt Debbi I would go to her house Friday after school. We are going to start getting the baby's room ready. We're picking up some supplies today. I can't cancel on her. She's counting on me to help, *and* she's giving me the drive to the city."

"Friday night my parents go out to play cards. I watch Mara, but you can come over to my place." I'd love the company and it was a great way to start March Break.

"Perfect, it's a date. I'll get my dad to drop me off Friday evening after supper. Are you guys going to school Friday? I talked my parents into giving me the day off. I explained what a joke this week has been and how all we're doing Friday in class is watching movies, so they agreed to let me stay home. As far as I know, almost everyone is staying home on Friday."

Nila and I looked at each other. "I don't know, Amber," I said. "I haven't asked my parents for Friday off, but if everyone else is staying home, I'll see what I can do."

"Hopefully, then I can come over earlier."

"I'll ask my mom too," said Nila. "I've already got this afternoon off, but she'll probably say yes."

"And girls," Amber reminded us, "Rusty's hockey game is Sunday night. We're all going, right? It's the playoffs."

"I'm in as long as your dad can drive us to the rink," I said.

"I thought I smelled booze off of him the last time he drove us somewhere." Nila frowned. A little bit of her aura disappeared and settled into her skin.

"He will give us a ride and he won't drink that night, I promise," Amber assured us.

"Shit! Look at the time, we are running late." We hustled to Mrs. Walker's class. We were moving pretty fast. So fast, we didn't even see her coming, but Amber and Ruby squeezed through the door at the same time.

"Eww, Beryl!! I touched her," Ruby exclaimed. "Gross!!" She mimed shaking dirt off her hand, then wiped her hand on Beryl's sleeve. Some of the kids in the class laughed, and she did it again.

Amber's face flushed as red as her overlay. I didn't need to see her diminishing aura to know she was embarrassed, and that Ruby had hurt her feelings. The entire class could see it.

Amber turned as if she was going to run back into the hall. Rusty was right behind us. He saw the whole thing! Amber's red face got even brighter, and her yellow aura retreated right back into her body. It was engulfed by her red overlay, which was the biggest and brightest I'd seen it.

"Settle down and take your seats everyone." Mrs. Walker got up from her desk and stepped to the front of the class to begin the roll call.

Amber avoided Ruby for the rest of the day.

That evening, after *Jeopardy*, we were lounging around the living room. Mara was playing on her blanket again.

"Look Mom, she's perfecting another yoga move. This time it's the child's pose." Mara had her feet tucked underneath her and her arms were stretched out in front of her. "This kid is amazing! We should put her on *Star Search* or something."

"Oh Violet, you're silly!" Mom said. Dad was sitting on the couch beside her. Their auras were the exact same size and shape. "You must be getting excited about March Break. It starts this Friday."

"Yes I am Mom! I can't wait to stay up and sleep in for a week straight. I don't plan on doing much other than some reading and staying inside from the cold. But it will be nice spending time with you awesome, intelligent, beautiful people!" I buttered them up, before asking for Friday off.

"Wow! Awesome, intelligent, beautiful!" Dad grinned, "What do you want Violet?" He was onto me.

"Funny you should ask, there is a little, tiny favor you could do for me. I would really appreciate it and forever grateful – Amber and Nila aren't going to school on Friday." I exaggerated a bit. "Most of the kids are staying home and Friday we are just watching movies." I was started to sweat. "So, can I stay home too?" I finished the last line as fast as I could. This was not the first time I had lied about school, but it made me more uncomfortable than it had before. I didn't know why.

Mom and Dad looked at each other and shrugged. Dad said, "I guess, we don't see any harm in it, as long as you're not going to be missing anything and all of your work will be done beforehand." Dad's demeanor changed and he appeared to soften. "Besides, you have been staying late after school, busy at the library, you deserve a break. You've been working hard and putting the extra time in." He smiled and his aura brightened.

I felt my cheeks warm and knew I was red in the face, but I smiled back. "Thank you, Dad! I definitely won't be missing anything on Friday, and I'll make sure any assignments I *do* have will be handed in early. Oh, and Amber is going to come over Friday night. If it's okay with you two." I decided to slip this request in while we were talking about the weekend, and they were being so agreeable. Not that they would ever say no to Amber. My parents love having her here.

"Amber! Seems like forever since we saw her last. Tell her to come over early, if she wants."

"Thank you!" I went upstairs and got ready for bed. I washed my face and brushed my teeth, put on my favorite pair of purple pajamas, and crawled into bed. My pajamas are a cozy fleece material, and they match Nan's purple and white duvet perfectly.

I decided to do mindful meditation, my version of it at least, before going to sleep.

I closed my eyes and adjusted my breathing to slow, deep breaths. I cleared my mind of all thoughts, which sounds easy, but it takes some practice. I pretend I'm not in my bed anymore. I am floating in space with the stars, in silence. I do not worry about the past here. I am not anxious about the future either, I just float.

Suddenly a rainbow shot up and appeared around me, I was inside the color Violet. This is new, I thought, confused. I heard my name being called from below. "Violet… Violet… Violet…" The voice was not the same as my previous dreams. It was a man's voice, strong and deep but at the same time he sounded gentle and kind. This authoritative voice was rising from the ground up into the sky. I sank down with the colors of the rainbow around me. I was part of the rainbow. I could feel the energy from the other colors rushing around me, individually and unified, with our potential running at full force. I was one with them. I was part of the colors, and the colors were parts of me, though I felt most connected to the color violet.

I traveled down for a long time, but I knew only minutes or seconds passed. My spirit returned to the form of my physical body. I was standing among the clouds when I stopped moving. Everything was complete, serene, still. The sunshine with the clouds is brilliant, and the sun's heat filled my entire being. My aura grew outward, it separated into rays, extending farther and farther away. Part of me felt dizzy, but I also had a clarity of sight and understanding. As though, I could see and follow the molecules of air dancing in a warm breeze around me. My skin tingled with pure joy.

The man I had heard calling my name was beside me. I turned around and looked up at him. This must be

Seven's mentor, I thought. He was old, probably in his seventies or eighties. His aura color was violet too, like mine, but even more spectacular than Seven's had been. There was an area of white light glowing directly above his head, almost like a second aura. He wore a robe that was white, or light violet – it was hard to tell with the intensity of his aura. The fabric shimmered as he moved.

"Violet, my name is Gabriel." He extended his hand for me to shake. The moment our hands touched, I could feel electricity shoot through me. It tingled and was soothing at the same time. The sensations continued afterwards and my hand stayed warm.

"I am here because I have information to pass on to you. You will gain an understanding which will enable you to help guide the rest of humanity." He took a deep breath. Bright white beacons of light in his aura became more profound and began to shift. "I will visit you three times. I am Seven's mentor. Please consider me your teacher too, and each visit from me a lesson." I nodded my head in approval. "Splendid! Tonight is our first."

"I brought us here to this rainbow." I looked around, smiled, and nodded again. "I see you are Catholic, maybe not religious per se but you have a personal relationship with God."

How does he know so much about me? I wondered. Were they watching me? Was it Seven and Gabriel that I was overhearing through the baby monitor?

"Have you ever heard the saying that God left rainbows as a reminder?"

"No, I didn't." I hadn't heard that reference before.

"It's true." Gabriel said. "Rainbows are very important. They are a covenant between the universe, people, and God but it's not black and white. There are many different perspectives to it.

"The white light above Gabriel's head grew brighter and brighter, his aura and robe became a deeper purple as he continued to speak.

"Most people think this reminder is that God keeps his promises and that he is faithful. While this is true, it's not the only meaning."

I took in the most heavenly scent as he spoke. It was a subtle vanilla, mixed with a floral, and whiffs of more exotic fragrances. I could not tell if it came from the rainbow we stood in, the clouds around us, or from Gabriel himself.

"Right now, in this rainbow, we are part of the color violet. A rainbow has seven colors, and each color represents people's aura colors. So, each row represents the people that correspond to that color."

I went over what he was saying in my mind. I think I understood what he meant.

"Now consider this. Have you ever heard, thou shall love thy neighbor as thy self?"

"Yes, I have. I remember it from my religion classes."

"So, what I am telling you is the reminder is not only for the people, but also about the people. We are supposed to treat others as we would want to be treated, and to work together as one. The results will be beautiful, like a rainbow."

The white sparkles in my aura grew larger and shone brighter than before.

"Violet, you know what I am talking about. I can see it. Deep down you remember everything, you ever knew and learned from your past lives."

I suddenly felt more confident.

"Now, Violet, your people are beginning the next phase of your evolution, the spiritual one. During this time, people will start working together. The labels people carry, some proudly, some not, will be dropped. People will live together, consciously, to create one life, resulting in one love." He paused, and his voice softened, "It will make your lives better." His halo grew to be the brightest white I've ever witnessed and yet his robe turned a darker, royal purple.

"A time is approaching, Violet, when people will truly and completely see one another, for who we really are. People will become aware that we are not much different from one another. Everyone has the same needs, and most have the same desires. We want for ourselves and our families, admiration, health, well-being, happiness, laughter, and love. When the time comes, you will appreciate the differences that make us individuals. We are all the same, in many ways, our differences make us unique. There will be a fresh understanding, a new-found acceptance that does not exist in your realm."

"You will see more people reaching out to help one another, lifting each other. It is time to build people up, to help them reach their potential, and to show them the beauty within themselves. It is there. I know it is difficult to comprehend, Violet, but your dimension is keeping most of us in the universe and even beyond, from functioning at our full force."

I watched in awe as the rays of light shining from his aura turned a pale yellow or white, to the different colors of the rainbow. They moved in orbit around him.

"You are an enlightened soul. It is by no mistake you are named Violet, and that you, my dear, are our first Auracle."

CHAPTER 14

Buzz! Buzz! Buzz! My alarm was ringing. I woke up feeling happier than I had before, or for as long as I could remember, that is. I had an inner peace I previously didn't have. Everything would be all right, no matter what. My vision was clearer, my hearing more sensitive, and even my breakfast tasted better. Several years ago, my parents used their income tax return to buy a new TV. It was a big 36-inch screen, with stereo sound. Everything looked and sounded crisper and cleaner. The morning was like that.

When I left for school, Nila met me on the path with a huge smile on her face. She was carrying a gift box. It was neatly wrapped in shiny blue paper with silver ribbons tied in a bow.

"It looks lovely Nila! What did you get for him?" I asked.

"I found this cologne on sale at The Bay. It's called Fierce by Abercrombie & Fitch. I think Rusty will really like it. It's supposed to smell sporty, and be bold, just like him." Nila was a beaming blue beauty.

"I am sure he will. It smells nice."

Nila looked confused, "Can you smell it? It sealed in plastic inside the box."

I didn't want to tell her I could, so I quickly added, "Sorry, it *looks* nice! Nice wrapping job."

"Yes, it really does, doesn't it? Thank you, but I can't take all the credit." Nila replied, happy with the compliment. "The sales lady at the store asked if it was a gift and offered to wrap it. I wish I could do something that fancy. I think Amber will like it."

As we walked to school, the sun seemed to shine brighter than usual. It was still a long way to summer, but there was not a cloud in the sky. It was blue for miles, like the ocean.

While Nila and I walked along the old train tracks, the rocks crunched beneath our feet. It sounded like they groaned when they rubbed against each other under our feet. I hadn't heard noticed it before. I knew the rocks hadn't changed, but now I could hear the individual pebbles shifting down or sideways, and the striking of each rough surface against another.

In the school, the auras, noises, and scents of all the individual students and teachers overwhelmed me. My eyes, ears, and nose began to twitch and felt itchy.

Amber met us inside the entrance of the school at our bench. She jumped up when she saw the gift. "Thank you, thank you, thank you, Nila! I cannot thank you enough. This is perfect!" Amber studied the outside of the box. "What is it?"

Nila and I laughed. "It's a new cologne, Fierce by Abercrombie and Fitch. It's sporty smelling. I think Rusty will really like it."

"Thanks again Nila! You saved me. I cannot wait to give it to him." Amber put the gift box inside her school bag.

By lunch time that day my senses were no longer overwhelming me, but strong just the same.

I sent Perry an email during computer class.

"Let's get together over the March Break for another meeting of the minds." I ended my message with a big smiley face for good measure. I hit send and watched Perry from my seat, same as I had before. This time he turned in his chair and nodded at me with a smile. That made me smile.

He replied, "Don't be scared to give me a call, 902-555-3195. I'm looking forward to hearing from you!"

I admit that Perry is on my radar. We haven't talked much but I'll give him a nod or wave when I see him. I like the idea of having someone I can confide in, with no judgment, and I am starting to believe that is Perry. I think he feels the same way. I'm eventually planning to tell Nila and Amber that he may not be as peculiar as we thought, and we should give him a chance.

Amber was freaking out by last break.

"I still haven't had a chance to give Rusty his gift. At first break he was with his friends, and he played intramurals at lunch time." Rusty walked by with Alex and Craig. Red sparks flew in bursts out from Amber's yellow aura. "Not again! Is he *ever* alone? I'm going to have to give him his gift later. I'll call him tonight to let him know I have it. Hopefully we can meet up before his birthday, maybe it will have to be after his hockey game on Sunday."

Amber's anticipation and nervousness was obvious in her aura. It was smaller than before, and her energy shifted nervously as it moved around inside of it. It looked like someone had thrown handfuls of glitter at her, which would shake and scatter quickly around her as she spoke, denser in some areas than others.

"Amber do not worry about getting the gift to Rusty, you just started seeing him. I'm sure he will think you are thoughtful when he receives it, and there's lots of time before his birthday." My words seemed to calm her down.

With so many students taking Friday off, the mood at school was upbeat. The hallways were louder than usual, and everyone was in a good mood, even the teacher's auras were bigger and brighter. Everyone was excited about March Break.

After dinner, I was alone in my room. I thought about how *different* I'd been feeling. I reflected as I gathered the notes I kept from my dreams, the information I printed from online, and my library books. It was quite the collection I was gathering. The stack of papers was tall in front of me, but I felt strong and energetic. Besides, there was no harm in staying up late since I was off from school the next day anyways. I read well into the night.

CHAPTER 15

Friday, after lunch, Amber's dad dropped her off at my house. We were going to watch Mara that evening while my parents went out playing cards, but they decided to leave earlier since Amber was coming over that afternoon. They were meeting their friends for a few drinks and supper before cards that evening. They too were taking full advantage of that Friday I had off school. They don't get many opportunities to do that.

Like most of my girl's nights, I planned an evening filled with gossip, movies, and munchies. That night's movie choice was *10 Things I Hate About You*. We had seen the movie before, obviously, it did come from the library, but Amber loves Heath Ledger and so do I. What red blooded girl doesn't? I knew Amber wouldn't mind looking at Heath for a couple hours even if she wasn't that keen on watching the movie again. He was her biggest celebrity crush, and she had a few.

I was surprised when Amber walked through the door carrying my yoga video.

"Yo didn't bring it?" I teased.

"Yo better believe I did," Amber joked back in return.

"I funny, you funny." I said in jest. "So, did you talk to Rusty about the gift?"

"I'll fill you in after your parents leave." Amber's aura glowed brighter, it was good news.

A vision of Rusty and Amber started playing in my head. They were standing outside Amber's house. She handed him the neatly wrapped blue box. He tore into the paper. It didn't look like he had appreciated the wrapping job whatsoever. Once he opened it, he gave Amber a great big hug and kiss, real big! I almost laughed out loud at the kiss. He came on so strong, it looked awkward and sloppy. He might have been drinking too since his aura looked dimmer and murkier than normal.

I was not sure if my vision was what happened, if it hadn't happened *yet*, or maybe it was just my imagination. I couldn't wait to hear from Amber. My parents seemed to take forever getting ready, especially Mom. While Dad waited, he and Amber chatted. He loves that she laughs at his corny dad jokes and seems interested in old stories from his glory days.

Mom finally took one last look around the main floor, making sure everything was in order for us girls before making her grand exit for the night. The last item on her mental checklist was to pick up Mara and give her a kiss goodbye.

"Have a great time, girls," Mom said, as she put her coat on, and opened the door.

Dad followed along close behind her. "Yes, have a good time you two, but behave! I don't want to have to fight any boys off when I get home." Dad loves to torment us.

My parents are two happy people who belong together. I can see it. I know when one of them is upset with the other, but it's always clear they are still in love. Mara and I are lucky to have them, unlike Nila and the other single parent families in the neighborhood.

"Bye!" Amber and I chimed in together.

"I thought they would never leave!" I exclaimed, after my parents got into their car and I closed the door.

Amber scooped Mara up. "Who's a pretty baby? You're a pretty baby!"

Mara laughed and cooed back at her. We walked into the living room and sat down.

"So, I saw Rusty last night!"

"You did! How did that happen?"

"After supper, I walked down to Sam and Steve's for some snacks." Sam & Steve's is a little store with a few grocery items, pizza slices, ice cream, and so on. It's a local hot spot for us teenagers, a place to hang out. They have a couple of pool tables downstairs in the basement. If you're a smoker, they sell individual cigarettes.

Amber continued her story. "I ran into Rusty, Craig, and Alex. We chatted for a few minutes, then Craig and Alex left for Alex's house." Amber's voice rose with excitement and the pace grew quicker. The white sparkles in her aura glistened and moved in waves. "Rusty asked if he could walk me home. When we got to my house, I told him to wait outside, that I had something for him. I brought it out and gave it to him."

I noticed a change in Amber's aura as she kept talking. It appeared to get duller, and her red overlay grew brighter. It wasn't that significant, but it was enough that I caught it.

"He said the wrapping looked so great that he hated to open it! But he did, and he loved the cologne! It was one he wanted to buy for himself! Then he gave me a really fierce kiss! See what I did there?"

I nodded, knowingly.

"I *really* do think that he likes it!"

Good for Amber! I was grateful that she'd been able to give Rusty the gift, and that he had liked it. I wondered if the kiss was as bad as the one I saw. I wanted to ask about it, but I didn't want Amber to suspect anything.

Before the movie, we changed into our pajamas. We were watching it on the TV in the living room since my parents were out. About halfway through, Mara got fussy.

"She's tired. I'll changed her and put her down for the night." Once she was settled, we got more snacks out, and continued watching the movie.

Despite Heath Ledger being the hunk of a man he was, I found myself studying my friend. I've always been impressed by Amber. I admired her, and maybe even envied her. Her pajamas, not surprisingly, were yellow. The color complimented her fair complexion. Her hair was pulled back, but a few loose blonde pieces had escaped the ponytail and framed her face. She's a combination of gorgeous and goofy. A beautiful and fun-loving soul, but her red overlay was still there and tonight I was going to get to the bottom of it.

After the movie was over and our munchies were gone, Amber and I went up to my room. It was late and we were both sleepy. I was surprised Mom and Dad weren't home from cards yet, but I didn't mind them staying out later than usual since I had company.

We sleep in my double bed, which sounds small, but it's normally plenty of room for me and Amber. Except for the nights she spends tossing and turning. Sometimes she moves around a lot in her sleep. When I go to Amber's house for the night, it isn't an issue. She has a pull-out couch in her room. It's yellow, of course. My room isn't near as comfortable or convenient, but it works fine when she or Nila stay over.

Once in bed, we lay there without speaking. It was unusual, it felt like we were both nervous about something we wanted to say. I was anxious, but I spoke first.

"Amber, we have been friends for as long as I can remember. I'm not sure what it is, but I have a feeling something is bothering you, besides Ruby. It's probably nothing but, if you *ever* need to talk about *anything*, I'm here for you. I'd never tell anyone else or judge you whatsoever. You can trust me."

I looked in Amber's eyes. She looked like she might cry, before she took in a deep breath, her overlay burned bright red. She released the breath as her aura withdrew tight back into her body. Amber hesitated for a moment. Then she began to speak.

"Violet, I am glad you said something. I guess, maybe since we have been friends for so long, you know me better than anyone else. I *have* been keeping a secret, something I've buried deep down inside of me for most of my life." I watched as Amber tugged at the sleeves of her yellow pajamas. Her red overlay seemed to spit fire. "Lately it's been resurfacing and even though I keep trying to forget about it, I can't. I'm not sure if you know this about me or not, and I don't really want to talk about it, but I have to confide in someone."

Amber looked like she was going to burst into tears, but she kept it in and continued. "Violet, my mother got with my dad, or um, my stepfather, when I was really young. They started their own family a couple of years later, with my little brother. I always feel like a bit of an outsider in my own home."

I was completely flabbergasted. What was Amber talking about? "I didn't know that, Amber." I didn't know what else to say, so I just listened.

"My real father left home when I was three. I remember asking for him, after he left, and my mom saying he'd be back. I waited for years, which is more than I can say for Mom. I know she started dating my dad shortly after. I always had the feeling he had his eye on her for a while. It seems like he jumped at the opportunity, you know, once my real dad left and Mom was alone." Amber's face was almost as red as her overlay and her eyes welled with tears. "Mom says she doesn't like to talk about him, but one time, she said my real dad had a lot of his own issues, bad ones. So awful that kept him from coming back home. That is why he left us, and never came back home. It wasn't because he didn't love us."

"I'm sure he loved you more than anyone else." I tried to comfort her.

"I never saw him again. I don't know if he is dead or alive. Hell, I hardly remember him at all. I guess he sounds like some sort of deadbeat, eh?" She didn't stop long enough for me to answer.

"I have this emptiness that I've tried to bury, but it's becoming more prevalent. I never understood it, but I never did forget. I just want to know why he left. I miss him, and it still hurts."

I couldn't imagine what Amber was feeling on the inside, but, on the outside, her aura changed. As she spoke her red overlay grew bigger and brighter until it had taken over her yellow aura.

I hadn't expected this from Amber, not now, not ever. I hugged her tight. "Oh Amber, I am so very sorry, I had absolutely no clue you were going through this. I do not remember your real father, I've never heard of him before, I swear."

After our talk, Amber and I lay in bed together, somber and silent. I felt terrible for her. I reached under the covers and found her hand. I held it most of that night. I don't know if it helped her or not. I hoped it did, I know it made me feel better. Amber fell asleep before I did. When we were young, Amber always hated to be the last one to fall asleep. I think she still felt that way but didn't vocalize it anymore.

My heart ached for Amber. She's my best friend and I didn't know her as well as I thought I did. She seemed to be someone who had it all. I was even jealous of the poor girl up until an hour ago. I had passed a judgment on Perry too. Yes, he is different, but I always thought of him as a peculiar person, a bit creepy too. He has always seemed like the odd loner, but as I get to know him better, the real Perry seems like a cool guy. There are probably so many misunderstood people on the planet, I concluded before drifting off to sleep.

CHAPTER 16

Sunday evening, Amber and her dad picked me and Nila up for Rusty's hockey game. Shortly after six, we were on our way to the rink.

The drive was only a few minutes from my house to the rink. Everything in Glencarter is close. We pulled up to the rectangle shaped building, in a line with other cars. The rink has an outer shell of steel blue siding. It isn't one of the prettiest sights in Glencarter, but it certainly is one of the most popular, especially during playoffs. I thanked Amber's dad as we got out of the SUV.

"Thanks for the ride," I said, stepping out of their new Range Rover. I still thought of him as Amber's dad, even though I knew he was her stepdad.

"No problem," he replied. "Anytime, Violet."

I don't know if I *really* looked at Amber's dad before that night, but I saw him in a new light. I could see why Amber's mom might have been attracted to him. He's handsome, for a dad, in an older rugged way. I'm sure he was much more handsome when he was younger too.

We met friends from school as we walked in and exchanged the usual pleasantries, "Hi there," I said, and "Should be a good game." Glencarter was playing their third game in the first round of their division playoffs. So far, it was two games to one, for Glencarter against their opponents this series, Big Pond.

Big Pond is a quiet town about an hour's drive south of Glencarter. I don't remember anything exciting happening there, ever. They aren't our town rivals, but we needed to beat them to advance to the next series.

The entrance to the rink leads directly into the canteen. I could smell the aroma of fast food outside, and it filled the room. We walked over and stood in line for some fries. As someone who hates skating and who has never been good at any sports, the only thing I like, I might even go so far as to say I love, about the rink are the fries. There is nothing better than an order of piping hot fries served in a cold rink. I enjoy mine smothered in ketchup.

We ordered our fries from a classmate's mom, Sheila. I see her almost every time I am here. Her son likes the same hockey team that my family does, the Toronto Maple Leafs. They haven't won a cup since the sixties. Most of the town are Montreal Canadiens fans. I think my mom used to work with Sheila back in the day. She's always super friendly to me. I don't think Sheila knows this, but she helps make me feel more at ease in a place where I am not really that comfortable. I don't fit in here. I don't understand what icing means or what being offside is. I can barely skate.

As we waited for our fries, the shimmer in Sheila's yellow aura seemed to separate and scatter. I was trying to figure out what it meant when I had an anxious feeling come over me. I saw Sheila staying up late at night, worrying about money. She works here, as a second job on evenings and during weekends so she can pay for Ryan, my classmate, to play hockey. He loves it and money has been tight since her husband's hours were cut back at the mill.

"Violet!" I looked up and Sheila was holding out the fries. "I know you love your fries! I have a joke, especially for you. Where were the first fries made?"

I shrugged my shoulders. "They are French, maybe France or Quebec."

"No, in Greece!" Sheila replied.

We laughed, but I could see sadness that I hadn't seen before.

I followed close behind Amber and Nila as we headed to the main arena through a large set of swinging gray doors. We walked into a sea of hockey jackets. There were almost as many fans and parents from Big Pond, supporting their Muskrats, as there were from Glencarter, supporting our Pirates. We found a few empty spots and sat down on the cool wooden blue bleachers.

AC/DC began playing, and everyone started cheering as both teams came out onto the ice. I could feel the energy from the crowd as both teams warmed up for the game, they were pumped. The auras in the arena were an assortment of the colors from my dreams. It reminded me of a bouquet of May flowers, only it didn't smell as good. Soon the music stopped, and we stood for the national anthem. Then the ref called the players to their positions for the puck drop. Rusty plays center forward, and he won the puck for Glencarter.

"Rusty is number two." Amber informed us. "It's his number in every sport he plays. He loves the number two outside of sports too." She felt the need to tell us all about his affliction. "It's after his birthday, March twenty-second. That's actually two twos. He told me it would be cooler if his birthday was in February, so it would be even more twos, but March is warmer. And he's looking forward to turning twenty-two, that will be his champagne birthday."

Amber talked about Rusty *a lot*. I agreed along with her, meanwhile hoping this wasn't going to become a trend. I enjoyed my fries as she rambled on and on.

Before I knew it, the first period was over. The score was still zero to zero. Riveting, I thought.

There was a brief intermission, with more music and announcements from local sponsors. The teams switched sides and the game continued. A few minutes passed into the second period, then Amber shrieked as Rusty went for a breakaway with the puck. He faked out their defense man, then stretched his arm far back and sent a slap shot hard into the net. He shoots, he scores!! I thought, as the crowd went wild. I could see sparks igniting, like fireworks, on the ice and in the stands as players and fans celebrated alike.

Glencarter won the game two to one. Rusty scored the first goal, and he assisted on the second one. Amber couldn't have been prouder as he was announced first star of the game. I wasn't surprised, and the Pirates were another step closer to becoming the season champs again this year.

"He really was great! Wasn't he girls?" I didn't know if Amber was asking us or reminding us, as her dad drove us home.

Amber's dad chuckled at her enthusiasm. "Oh, I'm sure he was, Princess."

I thanked Amber's dad as I got out, "Thanks again! I really appreciate it." I got inside my house. After the packed arena, I was happy to be home. The exposure to the different auras and scents were exhausting. Dad was still up watching TV when I came in. Mom and Mara were already in bed for the night.

"How was the game?"

"It was good, Dad. Glencarter won!" I said, before excusing myself for bed. "I'm drained, and cold. I'm going to go get under the covers. Good night."

I changed into my flannel pajamas and got into bed. I read over the pages I had scribbled in my notebook about the colors, and some printed papers I had in my nightstand on auras. I liked to review them when I had the time.

I was drawn to "The Key to the Colors." I had the characteristics for each color. I wrote them down after my dream, and I read it over and over ever since. Was there more meaning to them, more than what meets the eye?

I was pondering this idea when I heard a familiar voice in the distance. It was Gabriel. He was repeating our first lesson again. I listened as I drifted off into sleep. I wasn't sure if it was for my benefit or if I was overhearing him welcome another Violet.

CHAPTER 17

Over the next few weeks, it felt like things were changing. Amber, Nila, and I were starting to separate. Amber was spending more time with Rusty, and she talked to him on the phone every night. After March Break was over and we were back at school, she would sometimes hang out with him at recess and during lunch too. When Nila and I saw her, she talked about Rusty a lot.

I hadn't seen Rusty and Ruby interact much. Amber was almost always with him or keeping close tabs on him. Ruby seemed to be avoiding him, except for this one day that I couldn't shake. It was a couple of weeks after we returned to school. I had excused myself from computer class to go to the rest room.

"Thank you, Mr. MacClure." I said, as I stood up from one of the long desks of computer terminals that filled the room.

I left and walked down the hallway, and quickly took the corner toward the closest washrooms. I was surprised to see Rusty at his locker, talking to Ruby! As I walked by, I couldn't help but stare. I didn't mean to, but something caught my eye, something I would never have expected.

As I passed by, Rusty's aura looked shiny and bright. He seemed excited as the lights in his aura raced one another. I never saw him react this way toward Amber. Sure, his aura glowed for her, it got larger and shifted too, but nothing like this. Maybe I'm reading him wrong, I hoped. He is the only orange I know and besides, I know he likes Amber. He did invite her to the semi-formal, and she was stoked about that.

Most of the girls in my class were excited about the semi-formal. It is the last big dance in junior high. It's for the graduating class, but the grade eight students can attend too. There is no grand march, and you don't feel pressured to bring a date with you. Nila and I were planning on going solo, like the three of us did last year.

I wasn't excited about the semi. I was more interested in learning about auras. I was starting to talk to Perry more. I was spending less time with Nila, and I felt guilty about that, but I could talk to Perry about things I couldn't with Nila. Perry's comprehension of the supernatural superseded my own and I had a thirst for knowledge.

I was still waiting on another dream with Gabriel. I had a lot to learn. I didn't want to bring it up to Nila before I was ready, and I had some sort of understanding. I'd hate for her to think I was peculiar and maybe a little creepy, that would hurt. I wanted to have a significant understanding of this stuff before I brought it up with her. Meanwhile, I was spending more time with Perry than I had before.

We had not talked about it, but the initial awkwardness had become an easy relationship. Perry did not like to talk about himself, but he enjoyed having a friend. We discussed articles and books we had read. He shared some of his theories about the world with me, things he believed to be true. It was great to chat with someone about the future of humanity, the futility of war, and other important things, instead of who would win the playoffs or who would be king and queen of the semi.

Perry and I shared several classes, including biology, with Mr. MacDonald. Perry liked that class. He sometimes asked questions that seemed odd, but Mr. MacDonald was never condescending, unlike a few of our other teachers. He was younger, and still enthusiastic about teaching. He tried to encourage us to be curious about science. It could be overwhelming and exhausting, trying to keep up with him. Most of us tuned out, but Perry paid attention.

In biology class one afternoon, Mr. MacDonald was talking about photosynthesis. Then he got sidetracked into telling us about light. He reviewed the seven colors that make up the visible spectrum and are the components of white light.

"ROY-G-BIV is an easy abbreviation to remember the colors," he told the class. Then he listed them: "Red, orange, yellow, green, blue, indigo and violet."

I felt Perry's eyes on me from across the classroom. Was he thinking something I wasn't? If so, what was it? Obviously, these were the colors from my dreams. I knew that! Perry and I had noted them many times before, going over the aura colors and their meanings. These are the colors that make up a rainbow *and* white light too. There must be a connection, I thought.

That evening I called Perry. I wanted to know if I'd missed something in biology. If I did, was it related to auras? I had the feeling I did, and it was, and I didn't like it.

"Hey Perry, it's me," I said, when he answered his phone.

"Hi Violet," Perry replied. He always sounded excited to hear from me.

I got right to the point. I liked that Perry did not mind me being direct with him.

"In biology today, you kept looking over in my direction during Mr. MacDonald's lecture. Was there anything you came up with? Some sort of idea or a theory with the aura colors? I got this feeling today."

Perry cut me off he answered so fast. "Oh no, Violet, I just thought it was funny he was going over the same colors we talk about *all* the time. Nothing more, that's it."

I felt Perry knew I would be calling him. He sounded rehearsed and not too convincing. I pushed him a little further.

"Well, Perry, do you want to talk about it? Maybe there is more to it?"

"No Violet, this is something you should come up with, er, ah… think about," Perry corrected or caught himself, "on your own."

"Okay, thank you, Perry," I said. "You've been so much help. I'll call you when I figure it out. Bye!" I hung up. Why was he was being so secretive? I knew he wasn't being mean. I had a vision of Perry, smiling warmly, holding his phone.

I went to bed, obsessing about the class, reliving it in my mind. What was I missing? It's clearly something about the seven colors that make up white light. And Perry was testing me.

My mind was working in overdrive. I started to think about my Nan and the dreams. Was she connected? I wonder what Nan would think about me seeing auras and having visions. I looked over at her purple rosary hanging off my bed post. I'm certain she'd be happy, in a "that's my baby" sort of way. It brought me comfort and I felt better.

If I couldn't figure out the connection, I could at least get some sleep. Maybe I'll have a clearer head in the morning, and it'll make more sense then.

I said a prayer.

God, please lead me by your heavenly light and bring forth the clarity I need to see the path you have chosen for me, and please reveal any connections to the colors that I am meant to see. Amen.

I finally calmed down and was starting to doze off, when it came to me. I almost jumped out of my bed.

Each person is represented by one of the seven colors of light. The same colors that make up sunlight or white light. Since auras are light, what would happen if people came together and we united? Would the result be the equivalent of the colors of the spectrum producing white light?

It may sound complicated but it's actually quite a simple theory, when you think about it. If the people who make up the seven colors, which is everyone on our planet, all work together, if we unite as one – the conclusion could be a new color or creation and a new way of life for all.

I've heard people say that they follow a white light when they die, and they aren't afraid. I've also heard heaven described by the color white – people pass through the white pearly gates surrounded by white clouds and people in white robes with white halos above their heads welcome them.

People reaching the equivalent of the color white, would mean we will be in touch, or in tune, like my tuning forks, with a higher power or a greater force. It's something we are all striving for, whether we are conscious of it or not. It's something wise and pure, I just know it!

I felt proud. I figured out the meaning behind Perry's looks in class and realized a goal of our transition. I was beaming like a light bulb. I heard laughing and cheering, I presumed it was coming from the game my dad was watching on the TV downstairs. Despite the excitement of my new revelations, I felt at ease and quickly fell asleep.

CHAPTER 18

Nila and I met the next morning on the path for school, as per usual, but it felt different.

"Hi Violet."

Nila likes to call me Vi, Amber calls me Violet because she thinks it sounds more sophisticated, but Nila never does. She didn't use her pet name for me. I wonder if it's because she's noticed I've been spending less time with her.

Nila broke my train of thought. "I was talking to Amber on the phone last night. She wants us to spend Friday night at her place this weekend."

"Sure," I said. "It's been too long since the three of us got together for a sleepover. Sounds like fun!"

"I know! I can't wait! Although I am certain, we will hear what Rusty eats for breakfast Friday morning." Nila joked.

"*And* what he has for supper the night before." We laughed.

I hadn't told Nila about Amber's dad. I decided that is up to Amber to do but I also think Nila should know. It's hard to keep a secret from her, especially one this big.

Friday evening, Amber and her dad picked me and Nila up for the sleepover. As we drove up Main Street for Amber's house, I saw a streetlight burn out along the way, then another, and another. It was not unusual. No one else noticed, that was not unusual either.

"Thank you, Mr. Boertien," I said, as we pulled into the garage.

"Anytime, girls. It's always nice seeing you," Mr. Boertien replied.

Amber's house is larger and newer than any of the houses in the lower end. It is a huge white house with light gray stone trim. There are matching stone pieces that mark the end of the driveway.

Inside we were welcomed with a fresh citrus scent. We went through an entryway that led into a spacious white kitchen. Everything was top-notch. It was nice, but there was not much cooking done here. I knew Amber's dad went out drinking often, and I had a vision of Amber's mom eating alone with a stack of takeout boxes beside her. I didn't like the idea of eating in that room.

Amber's mom, Beverley, greeted us.

"Hello ladies," she sang out. Like Amber, she seems to almost sing when she speaks. She's also a natural beauty and another yellow. I guess it's in their genes. Beverley is a petite woman, and she always dresses in very fashionable clothes. I cannot remember ever seeing her without her hair and makeup done, and she exercises regularly. She takes care of herself. She doesn't work, so she has the time. My mom and Nila's mom are too busy working to worry about their appearance.

"You girls are in luck," Beverley said. "Little Petey is at a friend's house for a sleepover tonight too."

Amber's mom was referring to Amber's brother. He was eleven, a ginger, and a cutie, but he can be a little devil too. His favorite pastime is annoying the hell out of Amber. He especially loves it when we are over, so he can pester her company too. He knows that really gets to her. You can actually see his mind at work, looking from one thing to the next for anything that will get to Amber, and us too. He can be relentless at times.

Amber's dad followed us into the kitchen, grabbed a beer from the fridge, and headed for the living room to watch TV. We went up to Amber's bedroom. Her room is color coordinated with the rest of their house. It's painted white. Her room trimmings and furniture pieces are yellow. There is pale yellow, neon yellow and in-between yellow. It looks very pretty, and it suits her since she is sunny and bright.

I was looking forward to the three of us reconnecting. We spent time together at school and we talked almost every day, but not like we used to. It felt like we were growing apart. I didn't want that to happen to us and I thought it couldn't hurt to let them know.

"We need to do this more often," I began, "I miss hanging out with you two like this."

"So do I," said Nila. "Thanks for the invitation tonight, Amber.

"I have another invitation for tonight, if you are up for it." The pitch in Amber voice was higher and her aura became more energized. "Setting Day is Monday for the lobster traps, right? Rusty and a few friends are going to The Sugar Shack tonight for one final drunk before lobster season starts. They are going to hang out with his brother and some of their friends. I would love to go. It sounds like it will be a good time and there will be lots of guys there too. What do you think? Rusty's brother will pick us up."

Nila and I looked at each other. I was not keen on the idea, but Nila was all for it. I was outnumbered.

"Really!?!" Nila squealed, she scrunched up her nose and squeezed her shoulders together in excitement. "And Mike will pick us up?"

I could see her aura beaming, a brilliant blue at the thought of it.

"Oh yes, sure thing," Amber confirmed, "And I stole a pint of rum from my dad if you girls want to drink tonight."

Amber had a habit of stealing her dad's booze when he got shitfaced. I tried alcohol a few times when I stayed here before, and I am not much of a drinker. I don't have the stomach for it. One night ended with me having the dry heaves for half an hour. It was a good thing Amber's parents were out at a dance that night or we'd have been busted for sure. Nila, on the other hand, seemed to have a cast iron stomach. I once saw her eat a whole paper cup full of ketchup in a ketchup eating contest we had at Karen's Kitchen, a local summer takeout place. She can handle her liquor.

"Awesome!" Nila said.

"I'm going to call Rusty and tell him we're game."

We listened to Amber as she spoke on the phone to him. She put the phone down on the receiver. I could tell she was excited. "Mike's going to pick us up at eight. Let's get ready to go, we don't have much time!"

CHAPTER 19

After we finished our hair and makeup, Amber was admiring herself in the mirror. "We look great!" We were each wearing an outfit we found in Amber's closet. Nila could only fit into some of her active wear, but she managed to find a track suit that was too big for Amber. "Let's go downstairs and wait for Mike."

"Dad," Amber said, as we went into the living room to let him know we were leaving, "Ruby's sister is picking us up for a party."

I almost burst out laughing at Amber, Ruby really!?! She doesn't even *have* a sister.

"OK Princess, have fun." Amber's dad said, as he swallowed the last drink of beer from the bottle he was holding. He looked like he was getting a buzz. He seemed more relaxed, and his aura looked murkier than it was earlier.

At eight o'clock sharp, Mike pulled into Amber's driveway. We were waiting out in the front porch. Amber sang out to her parents. "Our drive is here."

Nila and I yelled, "Bye," as we left.

Mike drives an older, silver, Honda Civic. His best friend Austin was in the passenger seat. "Hi guys." Amber said, as we crammed into the back seat. The car reeked of Armor All and his stereo pumped out classic rock. The music was too loud to think, let alone talk.

We drove out of town toward the country road that leads to The Glen. Setting Day is coming up, and it's a good excuse for a party. It's the day the lobster fishermen in this area set their traps. My parents will both be working at the fish plant within the week.

Before Setting Day, there is excitement around my house, and in the town. You can feel it in the air. People are amped up! After a long winter inside, they are happy to be out, even if it is for work. They are tired of being cooped up inside, and the steady paycheck helps too.

Soon we were turning down the dirt road that leads into The Glen. We all know the way to The Sugar Shack, but us girls had never been to a party there, and our excitement grew with the growing darkness as we drove down the winding red road. We saw the old cabins and what we call parking lots, on both sides of the road along the way. Parking lots are basically open fields in the middle of the thick forest. People who don't own cabins park in them when they come out here to hang out or to party.

When we arrived at the small shack in the woods, the music was loud, and I could smell pot in the cold night air. Rusty, Alex, and Craig were inside. Each of them had a beer in their hand, and it looked as if it wasn't the first. No one was smoking a joint but their eyes, and the smell, were telling signs one was just put out.

"Hi handsome," Amber said to Rusty.

"Hey babe," Rusty shouted back as he reached over and grabbed her bottom. His aura looked dull, and Amber's red overlay grew brighter. He appeared to be drunk.

Amber did not seem to mind. Nila and I looked at each other, concerned.

"Amber, do you and your friends need a drink?" Rusty asked us, as he held up his glass, unsteady on his feet.

"Thanks, Rusty but we came prepared." Amber pulled the pint of rum out of her purse. "Well, almost. We do need a few glasses and some mix too, please."

"All on the table." Rusty waved at a table that doubled as a bar and rolling station. There were papers, liquor bottles, and two empty Coke bottles. No cups. Rusty looked closer at the table. "Hang on."

He walked over to the makeshift kitchen and dug through the old cupboards that lined unfinished walls. There was a row of empty hard liquor bottles on top of the cupboards. The counter was old, with burns in the plastic, and the sink had rust stains. It matched the rest of the cabin, old and filthy. There were several sagging couches around the room. The floors were plywood, stained dark from dirt and spills. The room was dimly lit, and a woodstove in the corner of the main room kept the place warm.

"Here you go." Rusty handed Amber a package of red plastic cups. Then he grabbed a Coke bottle, three quarters full, from an old green fridge stocked with beer, our mix. He put it on the table too, then said, "See you in a minute, babe. There is a song, I want to put on."

Amber poured a big drink for each of us. When she was done, the liquor bottle was half empty, and we had just arrived. Not that it mattered much to me. I didn't see myself drinking much more. I'd probably sip on this sucker the rest of the night.

Mike, Austin, and their friends were hanging out by the table, and they started to talk to us.

"So, you ladies will be in high school next year?"

"Yes, we can't wait. We are so over junior high!" Amber answered, as she took a big swig of her drink. It wasn't long before she was pouring her second. Then she walked over to Rusty. He was on a couch by a decrepit music system. Alex and Craig were by his side, Nila and I hung back. Rusty got a new song going and leaned back on the couch. Amber squeezed in beside him.

Mike and his friends started talking with some other people.

"Nila, do you want to sit down on one of the empty couches."

"I'd love to." We strutted over to a pale blue sofa and sat down. It wasn't comfortable, but better than standing. I scanned the room. Everyone's auras glowed. Some were bright in anticipation that helped light the room, while others were depressed from drugs and alcohol. We were nervous, I guess, because we got our drinks on quite quickly. Nila's was gone.

"Do you need a refill?" A friend of Mike's offered.

"No thanks, Amber has ours."

Soon my drink was gone too.

"Where is Amber? I don't see her anywhere." We looked around. Rusty was still on the couch.

"There she is," Nila pointed. Amber saw us and came over.

"Sorry, I was in the bathroom." She noticed our empty glasses, and promptly refilled them, the pint bottle was empty. "I hope you two are having as much fun as I am!" She went back over to Rusty, without waiting for a response.

Nila and I started in on the fresh drinks. Before I knew it, we were sounding like a couple of cliché old drunks.

"I love you," Nila said.

I slurred the words back to her.

"Violet, you are my best friend and, um, you know, you always will be… forever. You can always count on me, Vi."

"Same, Nila!" I agreed. "I feel the same way." Our auras cast out vivid colors of violet and blue in the dimly lit room like light houses in the night. Our insides were warmed with gratitude for each other, and by alcohol.

"I love Amber too," Nila shouted, as Rusty cranked up a Collective Soul song.

"Oh, me too, Nila," I yelled back at her. "We should go and tell her. Let's go and get her."

We started to walk, or rather stumble, across the floor, our arms locked and our knees weak.

"Amber!" Nila called out in Amber's direction. Amber and Rusty were together on a couch, not kissing, but close. "Amber!" Nila called again, a little louder than the last time.

Amber sighed and rolled her eyes.

"Amber, you need to come with us!" Nila declared.

"Not now girls!" Amber answered. "I'm with Rusty. I'll let you know when it's time to leave."

Nila and I looked at each other, dumbfounded. She couldn't leave Rusty's side for a few spare minutes for us. "We only wanted to tell you, we love you." Nila protested.

"And you have to tell me that right now. It sounds so childish. I told you, I'm with Rusty right now." He nuzzled her in closer.

Nila and I were pissed. Amber drug us both out here and had absolutely no time for us. I know she had a buzz, and she was trying to fit in, but those are not excuses to ignore your best friends. It made us furious.

"Come on Violet, let's go outside and get some fresh air," Nila suggested.

CHAPTER 20

As the time passed, more and more people arrived, crowding the cabin. We pushed past them to the wooden latch door to get outside. It was the end of April, and the weather was starting to get warmer, but the night air still had a bite to it. It normally would have made me shiver, but we were numb from the rum. I hadn't realized how smoky and loud the shack was until we walked outside.

A car pulled up the dirt road, turned in beside the others, and parked. A group of senior high school girls jumped out. They went inside without saying a word to me or Nila. Once they were gone, Nila began to cry. I watched the remaining sparkle disappear from her diminished aura.

"I can't believe Amber dismissed us like that, Violet. We are supposed to be her best friends, and it's like, she doesn't have the time of day for us!" Nila stumbled as she spoke.

"I know," I said to Nila. I wanted to say something to make her feel better. I wasn't ready to reveal my new secrets to her, so I blurted out Amber's.

"Amber's dad's not her dad!" I probably said it, partly out of spite. It was hard holding it in though, and the alcohol didn't help.

"What?" Nila voice echoed out into the night. "What did you say?"

I regretted telling Amber's secret as soon as I said it, but there was no taking it back. I told Nila everything I knew about Amber's dads.

"Mr. Boertien is actually her stepfather. Her real dad is some other man with even worse issues than him. A real deadbeat who left home when she was three. Her mom moved in with her dad, the dad she has now, almost right away. We would have only been two at the time."

"Oh my God!" Nila sounded almost sober.

"Don't say anything to Amber," I pleaded. "She told me a few weeks ago in confidence and I don't think I should have mentioned it." I felt sober too, and guilty.

"I won't, but I wonder why she never confided in me yet," Nila said. "I'm starting to get cold,"

"Me too. Let's go back inside."

The sofa we sat on earlier was empty. I pointed over to it. "Want to sit down on the couch?'

"Okay, I just have to run to the washroom first."

I sat on the sofa by myself, waiting for her to come back. After five mins or so, I was restless. I looked around, and I saw her talking with a couple of girls. They were a year older than us, and from the senior high school. They were in the car that had pulled up when Nila and I were outside.

What would they be talking to Nila about? I watched as one of the girl's slapped Nila on the back and another gave a beer. She's going to take forever. Amber was still snuggled up with Rusty, kissing on one of the couches. I could feel and see the energy of everyone in the room. I heard every word that everyone said but I felt alone, in a room full of people.

I wish Perry was here with me, then I wouldn't feel so alone. But then again, another thing Perry and I have in common, besides the supernatural, is that under normal circumstances, neither one of us would be found partying in The Glen. I'm surprised, I'm here. I should have just said no to Amber or have gone home. Instead, I felt sorry for her, and Nila really wanted to come. I could try to make new friends too but I'm not comfortable trying to socialize with everyone. I don't feel like making new friends, even with a bit of a buzz on.

"Violet."

The sound of my own name brought me back to the party. It was Craig. One of the popular kids was talking to me.

"Violet, do you want a beer?"

I knew I shouldn't, I figured I'd be sick. "Yes," I replied, "I'll take one Craig, thank you." It was Craig, and I was alone. He dug inside his cooler, then handed me a cold one as he sat down on the couch beside me. I can't believe he is talking to me. My aura grew brighter. I was happy to have his company but nervous. I knew him, but we never talked at school. I took a large swig from the bottle.

"Easy now," Craig joked.

"I am not much of a drinker, I swear." I said, as I took another drink.

"You're in a couple of my classes." He brushed his bangs out of his face. I could see Craig's green aura grow as he talked to me. I am not the type that gets into trouble with boys, but if I was, Craig could be one of them. He is tall, handsome, and he has that scar. Scars are hot. Green is a mental color so he should be more thoughtful than most guys our age. "I've always wanted to get to know you better."

"Yes, we're in a few of the same classes, Craig," I mustered.

"Rusty is seeing Amber now. She's one of your friends, right?" Craig questioned me as he moved in a little closer.

"He is," I smiled up at him. I wasn't sure how I felt about Craig, but it was nice having his attention. He was really cute too.

"Violet!" Amber was yelling my name. She saw us and ran over.

Now she knows me, I thought.

"We got to go, our drive is leaving." Nila had a bit of a stagger in her step, as she followed behind her. She must have had more beer, I thought.

One of Mike's friends was driving us home. Derek was one of the only sober people there. He has an eight am morning shift every Saturday at his grocery store job. There was plenty of room in his car since no one else was leaving the party yet.

"Okay Amber, thanks." I got up to leave.

Craig stood up too. "Bye Violet, see you at school."

"See you Monday, have a good night, Craig." I followed Amber and Nila into the night, in search of Derek's car.

"There he is," Amber pointed. "I'm going to get up front."

Nila and I crawled into the back seat. I looked at my phone. It was almost midnight. There were so many cars. I hoped no one was going to drive drunk. We didn't talk much on the drive back to Amber's house.

"Derek, do you mind if I look for a good song?"

"Go ahead, Amber."

Amber fiddled with his stereo, going back and forth between stations trying to find the song that she liked best. Then she turned it up loud and sang along to it. Derek didn't seem to mind.

Thank God, I thought, as we pulled up to Amber's house. I was beginning to get a headache between the loud music she was playing and her singing.

"Thanks, Derek." We chimed in together.

"Good night, ladies," Derek said. He turned up an Eminem song and drove off with the song blaring.

Amber's parents did not wait up for us. They never do. Once we got to her room, she clumsily pulled out the sofa bed for us.

"I'll make the bed." Nila reached for the extra set of bed sheets Amber keeps in her closet. I helped with the bedding before we got in. After we were all settled into our beds, Amber went over her night in detail. I passed out as Amber rambled on and on about Rusty:

"We got along so great tonight! Mike is nicer than I expected him to be. The Sugar Shack could have been cleaner, and Rusty's lips were so *soft*."

She never mentioned how she ignored Nila and me. But we did not forget.

CHAPTER 21

My stomach was squeamish on Saturday.

"Are you up?" Nila rolled around in the sofa bed toward me. "It's after eleven already."

"Really?" I replied. "I have to get home soon. Mom wanted me home early today. She has some stuff she wants to get done before work on Monday."

"I'll get Dad to drive you home." Amber piped up. "Can I get you something to eat before you go?"

"I'd love a bagel." Nila said.

"I think I can handle some juice." My throat was so dry.

Afterwards, Amber's dad dropped us off at my house.

I wanted to tell my parents I was sick with a stomach flu that's been going around, but I knew they would be onto me. Besides, the next day was Setting Day, and I didn't want to let them down, they were depending on me to help.

"Violet, I expected you home earlier." Mom said, as I opened the door.

"Sorry, we slept in." I frowned.

Mom handed Mara over to me. "Can you take your sister? I have so much to get done today."

"Come on Mara," I pulled her up on my hip, "Let's go into the living room and play."

By nightfall, I was exhausted. I didn't need to pray or meditate before sleep. I was way too tired to do either.

It wasn't long before I was walking along a busy street.

There were lots of people with me. I'm not afraid, I thought, this feels familiar, but I don't recognize the street or a single soul. This isn't Glencarter.

My old dog Sophie ran past me.

"Sophie!" I called after her, shaking my head in disbelief. As much as I wanted to see her, I knew it wasn't real. She died 3 years ago.

I am dreaming, I thought. A pulse of electricity rushed through me. I have no limits, not like I do when I'm awake. Here there are no restrictions, I can do anything, be anyone.

I tested my new environment. I bent my knees and squatted as low as I could. Then I sprung up into the air as high as I could. I shot up into the sky like a rocket with rainbow-colored flames coming from my feet. The air was warm on my face. On the way down, I could control my speed and maneuver myself. I darted back and forth across the sky above the street. I saw a sign hanging off one of the buildings. I stopped to read it. It was a quote, "Try to be a rainbow in someone's cloud." I had heard once that if you ever want to wake up from a dream, read something. Using your brain to analyze the words is supposed to require enough conscious thought to wake you up. As soon as I remembered that, I woke up.

I wrote down the date and the details from the dream. It wasn't one of my most memorable ones but the thing that made it special was that I knew I was dreaming. I never had a dream like that before and was not sure if I'd have another one like it. If I did, I'd record it too and see how frequent they are.

Sunday, I still wasn't feeling good. Maybe I was coming down with something. I shouldn't still be this groggy from The Glen on Friday, I thought.

We ate breakfast as a family. This would be our last one together for a few months.

"How many eggs do you want, Violet?" Mom asked.

"I'll have two please, over easy."

Mom passed me a plate full of food and I sat at the table.

We say grace sometimes when we eat as a family. It's almost always the same one, short and sweet.

God is good, God is great! Let us thank God for this food. Amen.

The day after Setting Day, Tuesday, Mom and Dad would be processing the catches at the plant. They'd be leaving home early for work. It was going to be my responsibility to babysit Mara before and after school. In the morning I'd drop her off at our neighbor's house, and pick her up when school is over. I'd be working almost as hard as Mom and Dad.

Monday morning, I met Nila on the path. We were both quiet as we walked to school. I didn't want to bring up Amber. I said enough to Nila about her Friday night. Even though Amber had been a bitch that night, I still felt bad about it. Nila's spirit was down that morning too. Her aura looked small.

"I'm not feeling good today, Violet," she said.

"Me neither," I agreed. "There *must* be something going around."

Because it was Setting Day, half our school was absent. There are plenty of kids whose parents are fishermen, and everyone helps on the boat that day. Some kids will go with an uncle or a cousin. It happens on Landing Day, too.

"Amber's not here today." Nila pointed to the empty bench.

She's not out on the boat, she never goes on Setting Day. It starts too early for her – 4am. Besides, it's way too cold on the water for her at the beginning of the season. She probably told her parents "No one else was going to be in school today." She seemed to be able to talk them into almost anything.

My first class was biology, Mr. MacDonald was talking about space.

"It's not part of the curriculum, and you won't be tested on it kids, it's just some really cool stuff. I want you to love science as much as I do."

He gets excited talking about it. His aura expands and expands like the universe when he does and his energy sparkles like stars in the sky. I usually enjoyed listening to him. Sometimes he sounds philosophical, like when he talked about black holes.

"Not much is known about black holes. One of the few things we do know about them is that one is formed, or born, when a star dies. Some people think it's a way to travel through time, and that the Bermuda triangle is one. Others think it's a tunnel, of darkness, leading to another time or dimension. No one knows for sure."

"I'd jump in a black hole," Alex bellowed, above the class. "Beam me up Scottie!"

The entire class erupted into laughter, except for me. I was still marveling about black holes and their possible meanings.

Mr. MacDonald continued. "Black holes might be related to the moment in time when our universe was formed. I'm talking about the Big Bang.

"Part of the theory is that during the Big Bang itself, at the moment of combustion, there was almost the same amount of matter as there was anti-matter." Mr. MacDonald made two fists and held them out in front of his chest, side by side. "These two components, you see class, are complete opposites of one another and when they meet, they cancel each other out." He crashed his fists together, mimicking the moment. "When the two were introduced to one another, there was an instant explosion." He spread his arms far apart. "There happened to be, the most-minute part more matter than anti-matter. And thankfully so, because the matter, that was left over, after the Big Bang occurred is our universe. It has been expanding and stretching over space and time ever since, becoming the universe as we know it today." Mr. MacDonald took in a deep breath, as if he'd run out of air from saying so much.

It sounded cool but it was a lot to take in all at once, totally overwhelming. I didn't fully understand it, but since we wouldn't be tested on it, I wasn't concerned about it.

That evening Perry phoned me. It was odd, because normally I called him.

"So, what did you think of biology today, Violet?"

I felt like I was having déjà vu. It wasn't that long ago since I called Perry about one of Mr. MacDonald's classes. Did I miss something again?

"I don't know, Perry, the part about black holes was interesting." I was tired. Mr. MacDonald's extra-curricular lectures can be a lot to try to take in on a good day, let alone one when you aren't feeling well. "Why? Did you pick up on anything Perry?" I figured it couldn't hurt to turn the tables on him.

"Nothing concrete, he was just really informative today, that's all."

He was calling me to tell me Mr. MacDonald was informative? Oh Perry please! Everyone knows that about Mr. MacDonald. I was certain Perry knew more than he was letting on. When it comes to breakthroughs, Perry likes to lead me, but he never gives me definite answers. I couldn't decipher the information then, so I told Perry about last Friday night instead.

"We went to Amber's for the night, and we ended up going to a party in The Glen. Almost everyone there was drinking. Amber was so busy canoodling with Rusty, she ignored Nila and me. We kind of let it slide, she was half drunk too, but it still stung a bit."

I didn't tell him about Amber's dads and how I told Nila the truth. I wasn't going to open my big mouth about that again, no matter what.

"Then Nila went to the bathroom and didn't come back. I saw her hanging out with some girls from high school."

"Did she know them?" Perry asked.

"She said they stopped to ask her if she was trying out for the basketball team this fall. They heard she was really good, then they offered her a beer, so she drank it with them."

"She is *really* good at basketball. She's one of the stars of our school team." said Perry.

"I know she is, and she's really tall too. So, I started to feel alone. I know it sounds silly, The Sugar Shack was packed. I was wishing you would have come too when out of the blue, Craig from our class approached me."

"Wow, Craig, really?" He sounded impressed.

"Yes Perry," I said, "But I wouldn't read too much into it. He was probably just being friendly or maybe he felt alone there too. I didn't see many people from our school." I told him, even though, I may have wondered once or twice since then, if there's a chance Craig likes me, I'm doubtful.

The popular boys don't go out with girls like me. I'm not popular or good at sports, and I'm not a natural beauty, or someone who wears makeup and does their hair. Besides, except for Nila and Amber, I was probably the only other girl there from junior high. Maybe he figured I'd make out with him.

"He'd be a fool not to fall for you, Violet."

I felt my internal temperature rise and my cheeks flush, "Thank you, Perry."

"I'm happy you made it home, safe and sound." He hung up the phone.

Later that night, I lay in bed, the seven aura colors flashed through my mind, over and over. Then I saw the sign with the quote from my dream, "Try to be a rainbow in someone's cloud."

It must be a message for me. When the colors align in the sky, side by side, a rainbow is created. They are beautiful, special, and rare but rainbows only come after a rain. The quote refers to someone's cloud, as though it's a dark and stormy time, when they are down and out. It is saying to be the human equivalent of a rainbow for someone else. A light during their dark. To be a sign they are not alone, do an act of kindness, a blessing in someone's life.

What would the conclusion be if we all united for the good of our planet and stood with one another, side by side, lifting each other up like rainbows? Could we create rainbows of sorts as a result? Maybe this will mark the beginning of our next era. A time equal to white light, a time of love, wholeness, and perfection.

I was overwhelming myself. I felt like Mr. MacDonald but instead of science, I was passionate about spirituality and the supernatural.

I was done for the night. I processed so much information, I needed to relax my mind. I didn't do this one often, but decided on a loving and kindness mediation. I always feel better after doing this technique. You can use yourself as the subject or someone else.

I relaxed my mind and muscles. I changed my breathing to long, deep breaths, my chest slowly expanded and decompressed with them.

I pictured Amber in my head. She was sitting on a bench at the park, it was a sunny day. She looked happy and she didn't have a red overlay anymore, it was gone. Her aura was a splendid yellow that was almost gold, it was large and sparkly. The park was full of people, but I didn't recognize anyone. She was not in Glencarter.

A puppy ran over to Amber. She picked it up, placed it on her knee, and petted it. The pup kissed her cheeks. She became happier and even more radiant. A small girl, with blonde hair that resembled Amber, took her by the hand. "I'm your inner child, let's go play." The little girl sounded like Amber too. It sounded like she sang when she spoke too.

The two of them ran over to a swing set, sat down on the canvas seats, and held onto the chains. "Let's see who can get the highest." Amber's inner child said.

I looked on as they laughed together. Amber was happier than I ever saw her before.

"Sorry, I have to stop," Amber said to the little girl. "It'll just take a second."

Amber drug her feet in the sand below her swing until she stopped and then she looked me dead in the eyes.

"Thank you for this, Violet. There is power in positive thinking."

She can see me? I looked down and saw myself. Instead of envisioning Amber, I was standing in the park with her. I'm asleep, I thought, I'm dreaming now. "You can't stay here. He's waiting for you, over there," she pointed, "under the sign."

"Okay, thank you Amber. I hope you have fun!"

She started swinging again and I started walking along the street from my dream the night before. I came to the building with the sign. I didn't see Gabriel. I jumped up into the sky for a better look. The rainbow rockets returned under my feet. I stopped at the sign and read the quote again, then I scanned the street below until I saw Gabriel ahead on the road. I descended toward the ground.

"Gabriel!" I shouted as I glided down to meet him.

"Hello Violet." Gabriel extended both of his arms out and embraced me.

What a rush! It's hard to put the feeling into words, but it was like a warm meal on a cold winter day while riding the most exhilarating roller coaster. Heat spread from my skin to my stomach and throughout my body at a high speed. I felt my stomach churn then I felt full. I knew I was still asleep, but I was more woke and alert than ever before.

"That is a hug!" I said to Gabriel. He smiled.

"Violet, let's walk along this road together, side by side." We talked as we traveled the long road. "Your second lesson is already underway. It has to do with your dreams."

"Every night when you dream, you are yourself, but your reality is different. It is not the same one you are in when you are awake. You wake up and return to your normal reality every morning. Sometimes you consciously remember your dreams from the night before and sometimes you do not. But they all have meaning. They do matter."

His energy shifted in dazzling white lights that looked like fiber optic lights shimmering in Gabriel's magnificent violet aura. Some were different sizes, the larger ones reflected light like strobe lights in the colors of the rainbow. They multiplied as he moved.

"There are different theories about dreams. That dreams are your true reality and when you are awake, it is the dream. Another is that you are every person in your dream, while others say your dreams develop from perceptions of your awake mind. All these theories have merit and are true to some degree."

"People receive messages in their dreams. These are from your own conscience or your spirit guides such as loved ones and angels. These messages help guide you on your path through life. People do not use their dreams to their full potential anymore, or their angels either. But that would be a completely different lesson." Gabriel laughed, as the lights shone bright in the sunlight and gold sparks ignited out from the white light around his head.

"The dream you had here last night, Violet, was a lucid dream. That's when you are dreaming and are conscious of it. You are asleep, but your mind is awake. You ask questions, like, 'Is this real? Could this happen? Is it an illusion or a dream?'" The lights in Gabriel's aura shifted around and formed the shape of a dove. The dove came to life and flew off into the sky as white electric currents moved through the halo above Gabriel's head like lightning. I watched with great reverence. Gabriel continued as though nothing had happened.

"Violet, in these dreams, because you are aware that it is a dream, your possibilities are endless. You've had that realization yourself."

I knew exactly what he had meant. I had tested the boundaries.

"You will start asking yourself more questions during your waking reality too, as you begin to change your own life. Violet, what is the difference between this dream realm and your awake reality? What is keeping your dreams from becoming your truth?"

I looked up into Gabriel's hazel eyes, knowing he held the secrets of the universe inside of him.

Gabriel put his hand on my head and my whole body felt warm. I had the same invigorating feeling as before. I closed my eyes, this time instead of the heat, I started moving at an extremely high speed. I felt dizzy until, I suddenly stopped. I opened my eyes, and I was back in my bed. I looked over at my alarm clock. It was time to get ready for school.

CHAPTER 22

Tuesday morning was hectic, and I should have been stressed but I felt lighter, I had a pep in my step. Mara was awake, cooing in her crib, when I went in to get her.

"Mara, you didn't cry when you woke up. You are such a good baby." I gave her a bottle, changed her diaper, and got her dressed in the clothes Mom left out.

I'm better at this than I thought I would be, I concluded, as I placed a few bottles Mom left for Mara in her baby bag.

After getting ready in what I considered to be record time, for the first day, we headed for the sitter, Sue. She's babysitting a handful of small kids from the neighborhood during fishing season, all under the table of course.

Sue lives in an older modest house on the corner of our block. She is a short heavy-set woman in her early fifties. She's always smiling, and she has a great sense of humor. Her laugh is bigger than she is. She is not strict with children, some may even say she is a little slack. But you can tell she loves the kids, and she has the patience of Job.

I knew Sue well enough that I walked inside without knocking. Sue's house is tidy but in an un-kept sort of way. She mops the floors daily, but they never look clean for long and there's lots of clutter. It's the complete opposite of Amber's house but with that being said, I would not like eating in Sue's kitchen either.

"Violet!" She exclaimed when she saw me. "How's baby Mara this morning?" She took Mara from my arms.

"She's great!" I said. "Here, Mom has everything you'll need for her today in this bag." I handed her the baby bag too. "I'm going to go, it's almost time to meet Nila."

"Have a great day, hun. I'll see you after school."

Nila was waiting on the path, beaming like a beacon in the night. "You will *never* guess who called me last night?" She sounded ecstatic.

"Who?" I asked. I was getting excited for her.

"Ava and Kelly called me on a three-way last night! They were a couple of the girls I was talking to at The Sugar Shack last weekend. They invited me to a girl's night at Ava's house this Friday." Nila was so stoked, the sparkles in her aura were vibrating.

I was surprised how fast they added her to their group. These high school girls don't waste time.

"That is great," I said to Nila. I wanted to be happy for her, and I tried to sound sincere, but I already felt like we were drifting apart. This wasn't going to help.

We met Amber at school, and I could tell she was nervous when Nila shared her news.

"*Really!?!*" was Amber's initial reply. She looked more shocked about Nila's news than I had been, but much less enthusiastic. "I hope it's not to get back at me!" I watched as Nila's aura dimmed. She didn't mention it to Amber again the rest of the day.

After school was over, I hustled to pick Mara up from Sue's. I didn't want to be late on the first day.

"Hi Sue," I said, when I went inside. She was putting away some of the toys the kids had played with that afternoon. Mara smiled and reached for me, I scooped her up.

"She had a wonderful first day! She ate well for me, and she had a nap. Mara even made a few new friends today." Sue said as she straightened up and wiped her brow. "I hope your parents enjoyed their first day back and the catches are plentiful this year."

I put Mara's coat and boots on her, and Sue gave me her baby bag.

"See you sweethearts tomorrow."

Mom had leftovers in the fridge for supper. They arrived home shortly after seven.

"Day one down!" Dad looked over at Mom and then down at his watch. The plant had started work at seven in the morning.

"Yes, Carl! We made it through the day. I'm not used to working like that anymore. It will take a couple of weeks to get used to it again."

Mom took off her shoes and collapsed on the couch.

Mara started crying when she saw Mom and Dad. She'd missed them. She reached her arms out and Dad picked her up.

"How was your day, Violet?" Mom asked "Did you have any problems with Mara? How did she get along at Sue's?"

"She was good this morning and Sue said she did great there, too." I didn't tell her I was tired. I knew they had enough to handle already. They had a hard day. I could see it in their auras. They were both lower, and lighter in color than normal.

I assumed they regretted wishing for this day to come. I knew we needed the money though, and they were happy to be earning a living again. I had a vision of them going to cash their first checks. Their spirits will be high on pay day, with their auras glowing bright on their way into the bank.

"I'm going to study." I excused myself and went to my room.

I called Perry to tell him about my dream the night before. He sounded interested in what I had to say.

"Do you think this relates to what we've been learning in Mr. MacDonald's class?" he asked.

"I really hadn't had a chance to think about it, but there must be a connection." He was giving me another hint, I knew, but I still didn't know what he meant. There was no point in trying to pry the answer out of him. So instead, I told Perry about Nila's plans for Friday night.

"There is certainly never a dull moment with you girls, Violet," he said. "I just hope Nila knows what she is getting herself into. Sorry, I got to go, Maxine is at my door and she's crying."

CHAPTER 23

Ring, Ring, Ring. I placed Mara in her playpen to answer the phone.

"Hello."

"Hi." It was Amber. "How's it going?"

"I'd be better if I didn't have to babysit today. I'm tired and I had to get up with Mara again this morning." I yawned.

"Oh shoot!"

"Why? What's wrong?"

"Rusty has a hockey game later. I really wanted you to come with me."

"Sorry, I can't. My Saturdays are pretty much booked until fishing season is over. What about Nila?" I had tried calling her earlier to hear how her night went with the high school girls but there was no answer.

"I'll ask her." Amber sounded hesitant about it. "There's only a couple of games left."

"I know! I'll come next time, if I can, I promise."

That afternoon I still hadn't heard from Nila. By then, I was dying to hear what happened at Ava's. After I put Mara down for her nap, I gave Nila another call.

"Hello," Nila sounded tired, and her throat was hoarse. I think I woke her up.

"Sorry, I hope I didn't wake you up." I had a vision of Nila sitting up in her bed and stretching. "So, did you have fun? What did you guys do?"

She cleared her throat. "Ya it was good, so Zack, Kelly's boyfriend, picked me up after supper to go to Ava's."

"Zack picked you up?" He's one of Ruby's older brothers. I was surprised, but I guess I should have expected that since he is Kelly's boyfriend. I wondered how Amber would feel about it.

"Ava's parents were out of town and a bunch of girls were already there by the time I arrived." She started rhyming off girl's names. "Ava, Kelly, Justine and Melissa, then, I saw a big bottle of vodka on the table."

That part didn't surprise me. I assumed there would be drinking. They are older high school girls.

"I was just sitting down, when Ruby and Beryl walked in from outside with a couple of drinks. Zack brought them and he'd left their cooler out on the front deck."

I almost fell off my chair. My knees would have buckled if I'd been standing up. "And then…" I prompted her for more.

"I couldn't tell you the last time that we talked, but last night they came right over to me. They were splitting a box of coolers Ruby's oldest brother bought for them. They both opened one and offered me one too, so I took it."

"That was nice of them." I grit my teeth.

"It started out innocently enough, I swear," Nila sighed. "We talked about the lobster catches this season, and how good they've been so far. Then, they told me how much they really like me, but that they never have a chance to talk to me because Amber's always around. Violet, they cannot stand her! They think she is such a skank."

I already knew that Ruby didn't like Amber. She'd been trying to sabotage her relationship with Rusty for months.

"Ava heard us talking and she joined in on the conversation. She said, Amber messed around with Justine's man a few months ago. He knew Amber from a friend of his that she dated a couple of times, and he ran into her at Sam & Steve's one night. She said, they ended up in one of the parking lots in The Glen and they'd been drinking. It got back to Justine, and she confronted him, but he told her nothing happened between them. Justine doesn't believe him, and she's had a hate on for Amber ever since."

Thank God for my chair! I was weak. "For real?"

"Yes, Violet! Amber's not that innocent. Toward the end of the night, I was sitting with Ruby, Beryl, Melissa, and Justine. They started talking shit about Amber again and then out of the blue, Ruby says her mother told her that Amber's dad isn't her real dad. Everyone was shocked, everyone except for me."

"No, you didn't Nila! Please! Tell me you didn't!" I felt the color run from my face.

"I am *so* sorry. I didn't mean to say it! I never would have, if I wasn't drunk, but I blurted 'I just found that out!' Everyone turned and looked at me. I couldn't deny it at that point, Violet. I told them it was true. Justine said that was confirmation for her. Then they started laughing at her and calling her names, like a skeez and my ex-best friend gone slut."

I was dumb founded. They tore poor Amber apart.

"Everything after that's a bit of a blur. I know Zack drove me home with Ruby and Beryl. I don't know what time I got in. Luckily, Mom had a few last night, so she didn't wake up or I'd be grounded. I've been napping off and on all day, but I still don't feel good."

"Go back to bed and I'll talk to you later."

I wanted to call Amber, but I didn't. I wasn't sure what to say to her.

"Wah!" Mara woke up, time to get her. I tried not to think too much more about Nila and Amber for the rest of the day. It wasn't that hard. I was busy with the baby.

Mom and Dad got home late.

"I know you're both really tired" I said "So, I'll change Mara into her PJs and put her down in her crib."

"Thank you so much, Violet! I'm exhausted." Mom's aura lit up and she gave me a hug.

After Mara was settled, I went to my room and got into bed. I was tired too.

Instead of thinking about Nila and Amber, I thought about outer space, black holes, and the Big Bang Theory. What am I missing? I yawned and stretched. My hand brushed Nan's rosary beads that I kept on my bed.

I wonder what she would say, if she was still here, if she hadn't died already. I don't want to die, I'm afraid of death. I like to think it's similar to birth, in that I won't realize or remember it. But I worry it's going to be traumatic and much more awful. The stuff nightmares are made of, I'm almost certain of it.

I heard before that it's common for people who've had a near-death experience to say that they traveled through a tunnel, reliving their past as they moved toward a white light. I wonder if it hurts? Is that what happened to Nan?

It was then that I had a light bulb moment. The theory of this tunnel reminded me of Mr. MacDonald's lecture, the one about black holes. That was the same day Perry called to tell me how "informative" Mr. MacDonald was, like I didn't already know.

He had said black holes are created when a star dies, and some people think it could be a tunnel to a different time or dimension. I remembered dreaming of being in a tunnel the night I met Seven too. They must be important.

Could there be a connection between an individual dying and a star dying? Furthermore, can a black hole be the equivalent to the tunnel one travels toward white light when passing over into the afterlife, from this dimension into another?

Could the same logic that applies to individuals apply to planets, stars, and maybe even the universe itself? I felt like I was getting closer to completing the puzzle.

I knew Perry would appreciate it. I called him to tell him about my epiphany. He was elated.

"You are on fire! I can totally see where you're coming from, I just wish I'd thought of it first. Keep it up! You are almost there!"

"What?" I questioned Perry. "I am?"

"I don't know for sure, I just have a feeling!"

After we hung up the phone, I lay back down in my bed. I was comforted by the idea that I was finally onto something. I stretched my arm above my head and my hand swept over Nan's purple prayer beads again.

I immediately started connecting more dots between the thoughts flowing through my mind.

Nan passed over from this realm to another one. The idea is quite trippy when you first think about it but the theory is more common than you might think. It reminded me of my lucid dreams and the two realities I experienced, my waking and sleeping ones.

In those dreams, any thought or idea I had was possible because every variable was working together under me. It was my dream, my ideas that I was acting out, with my own energy, leading to my purpose. I was in complete control of everything within that dream or reality because I was the only deciding factor. Therefore, all the energy was focused on the same action, working toward the same end.

What would happen if I applied this logic to life on our planet? In our awake or conscious reality, every person uses their energy to serve their own goals, and for the most part we operate as individuals to our own ends. Because of this, our cumulative energy as people is not stable, it's focused in different directions, with different goals in mind.

What if we changed that and we all decided to work together as one? Would anything be possible – things that we cannot accomplish today as individuals? The potential for what humanity could do if we worked together was out of this world.

I was proud of myself. Nan's purple prayer beads fell to the floor. I picked them up and put them back on my bed post. I was comforted. I felt like she already knew what I had just realized about black holes and lucid dreams. I thought I'd figured it out on my own, but maybe I didn't, maybe she had helped.

CHAPTER 24

Monday morning, I was happy to hand Mara over to Sue.

"It's so good to see you, Sue," I said, as her storm door slammed shut behind me.

"You look tired, Violet," Sue said, seeing it on my face.

"I am," I sighed, "but it will be worth it on payday."

"Another day, another dollar." Sue smiled. "I hear the catches have been good. It looks like everyone at the plant will be busy for the next couple of months."

"The catches have been good, better on the south side than the north side of the island, so far this season." I said. Mom and Dad keep me updated on the catches.

It's great news and the biggest in the town. Glencarter is on the south side of the island, and good catches mean more money and happier people.

"You are taking on so much responsibility, you will be old before your time. It's not so bad. It's mostly walking around wondering what you're forgetting." Sue let out a hearty laugh.

"I bet!" I laughed along as I agreed with her.

I left for the path to meet Nila. The sun was shining and it felt warm on my face. It's finally beginning to feel like summer is coming, I thought. I'm really looking forward to some lazy beach days, some me time. Although it will probably be me and Mara, I'll have to babysit!

By spring, I crave the ocean. It happens every year, especially after a cold winter. No matter how mild the weather, our winters are long, and linger well into the spring.

Being an Islander, I feel a natural connection with the sea. I love being close to it, being in it, and the smell of the salty air. I have no qualms about picking up a jelly fish or trying to catch amphipods, those small shrimp-like creatures that inhabit the tide pools during low tide.

Then there are beach areas only locals know about. When you walk down to the end of the town beach, where the rock begins, and turn the corner around the cliff-side, you are at Crab Island. That's what we kids call it, anyways. It is overrun with crabs after high tide.

If you walk the opposite way up the beach, you end up at The Hole. We were prone to undertows here. Years ago, as a safety measure, the beach in Glencarter was protected with small stone walls that run opposite to the shoreline to break the tide. They are called breakwaters and they prevent large currents from coming in. Along one of these walls far up from the main entrance to the beach, The Hole, was formed from an ocean's currents ebbing and flowing.

The Hole itself is only a few meters in diameter, and depending on the tides, it can be anywhere from just above your knees to chest deep. At low tide The Hole works as a natural hot tub. The shallow pool water warms up with the rising temperature and the sunshine.

If you are at all familiar with swimming in the Atlantic Ocean, you know that by the time you are waist deep, the water is getting cold below your knees. The cold progresses to the top the further out you go. The Hole is a nice alternative. The water is always warm there. The Glencarter kids love it! Knowing these spots is one of the perks to growing up here on the island.

Nila was standing in the sun, waiting for me at the path. A blue hue reflected off her raven-colored hair.

"You are beaming," Her aura looked bright and extra sparkly.

"Thanks, Violet! Same!" Nila sounded more chipper than usual too. She looked proud as a peacock. We started walking to school.

"Guess who called me last night?"

Oh no! Not again, I thought. I wasn't sure who it was, but I had a bad feeling in the pit of my stomach. "Ava?"

"No, Ruby!" Nila responded.

Oh my knees, I thought. Where is a chair when I need one!

"Who?" I wasn't sure if I needed her to confirm the name or if I was buying extra time to process it. Either way, I didn't want to believe it.

"Ruby," Nila confirmed.

"What did she want?" I asked.

"She was just saying how much fun she had with us girls Friday night and how cool it was to *finally* get a chance to talk to me, you know, without Amber being around. Beryl joined the call and she enjoyed herself too. She didn't say much at Ava's, so it was hard to tell. She only sipped on one of the coolers they brought. I guess Beryl doesn't like to party too much."

I was speechless. Nila continued.

"Anyway, Ruby said she is going to try out for the basketball team next year too. Her brother's girlfriend Kelly will be captain of the team next year. Then she asked me to go to the Pirates final playoff game with them on Friday."

I was floored. "That was so *nice* of Ruby." I said, sarcastically. "You're not actually going to go, are you?"

"Of course I am! Are you trying to say that you wouldn't go, if they invited you?" Nila eyes narrowed on me.

I wouldn't, I shook my head no, "Definitely not!"

I knew Amber wouldn't take Nila's news well either. Nila used to go to Rusty's hockey games with her, before she started hanging out with the high school girls. Amber was going to be pissed.

We met Amber at school. Things were different between her and Nila. Something was off, Amber felt it too. I watched her aura shift and her red overlay burn a brighter red than I had seen before.

Nila reluctantly told her about the phone call she received from Ruby.

"You wouldn't!" Amber was almost shouting. Her facial expressions gave away the hurt that I was seeing in her shrinking yellow aura.

"Sorry, Amber, but I told her I would go," Nila softly replied, as she lowered her head.

Amber's face dropped and she clenched her fists so tight her knuckles turned white. Red ignited out like lava from her overlay.

"Really Nila, Ruby? But you're one of my best friends and she's just using you to get back at me! You are so desperate!"

Yikes! I thought. "Stop!" I attempted to break the argument up.

"Sounds just like you and Rusty, Amber? Am I wrong?" Nila ridiculed her. Red and green sparks shot out from Nila's aura. "I think I hear Rusty's zipper rattling."

"Bitch!" Amber hugged her books tight to her chest and ran down the corridor toward the washrooms.

"Nila, what in the hell is wrong with you?" My rudeness was a knee-jerk reaction to seeing Amber upset, but I meant it.

"Please, Violet! What do you think? You're right, and everyone else is wrong about Amber? Open your eyes!"

I could feel my eyes. They were open and they were stinging. I headed for the washroom. I could hear Amber crying when I walked inside. I checked the other stalls and no one else was there.

"Amber," I whispered, standing on the other side of her door. She slowly opened it.

"Violet," Amber was relieved to see me, and we embraced in a huge hug. I could feel her energy embrace me too. "You are my one true friend."

CHAPTER 25

I really wanted to go to the hockey game with Amber. She needed my support. The Friday night games are later than the Saturday ones, so I figured my parents would say yes. I asked Mom while we were washing the dishes after they finished supper.

"Mom, the Pirates final playoff game is this Friday. The game starts at 7:30, you and Dad are almost *always* home by seven or shortly after. Can I please go? Amber's dad will drive us."

I dried the plate Mom had passed me and put it in the cupboard. Mom finished washing another and rinsed it before she answered. I could see in her aura she was pondering the idea. The energy or sparkles were shifting into different positions. The size and color of her aura didn't change, so it didn't look like she was against it.

"I'm sure we can make that happen. I'll tell my boss our babysitter has to leave at seven. You have been doing a great job, and I don't think she will mind us going home a few minutes early either."

"Thank you, Mom!" I gave her a hug.

Friday evening my parents arrived home at seven o'clock as planned.

"Yay! You made it." I said, as they walked through the door.

"Yes, and we didn't even have to leave work early."

"Awesome!" I took Mara upstairs while I got ready. It didn't take long, it was basically a quick hair brush and an outfit change.

Mom was heating up supper when I heard the car horn. I put my coat on to leave.

Mara threw her bottle on the floor. It's a game she likes to play with us. I spent the last few hours picking it up and giving it back to her. It can be annoying, but it keeps her happy.

"I gotta run!" I picked the bottle up and gave it back to her one last time before I left. "See you guys later."

"Hi Violet," Amber said, as I got in the car.

"Nice night," Amber's dad said.

"Hello. It sure is."

I could smell alcohol in the car as we drove up Main Street. Amber's dad dropped us off at the entrance to the rink.

"I'll call you when the game is almost over, so you or Mom can come get us."

I hoped to see Beverley since I thought I caught that whiff of alcohol off Amber's dad's breath. I thanked him for the drive anyways, because I always do.

The parking lot was packed full. I would have been able to smell the rink fries outside even without my sharper senses that I'd been having since I started seeing auras. Amber and I walked inside. The rink was like the parking lot, packed. I had never seen the rink so full.

We made our way to the canteen and ordered some fries from Sheila.

"The usual, Violet?" She smiled. There was no time for jokes. The line for the canteen was long.

"Yes, please!" My hands touched Sheila's as she passed me the fries. I could feel that some of the tension was gone and I knew her husband's hours were increased at the mill.

I loaded my fries with ketchup before we looked for a seat. We walked through the gray swinging doors into the main area of the rink. The cold in the air, from the ice, gave me goosebumps. The blue wooden bleachers were crammed with people. The stands looked more like a Picasso painting than a rainbow, and the crowd was electric. The place was lit up like a Christmas tree.

Everyone was excited for the game to begin. Amber and I stood beside the swinging doors scanning the rink for a spot to sit down. I saw lots of people from Glencarter, and lots I didn't know, from out of town. I caught sight of Nila and Ruby out of the corner of my eye, up in the top stands near the opposite end of the rink. That's where all the cool high school kids hang out. The only time I watched a game there was when I went to one of little Pete's games with Amber. His games didn't draw crowds, so there weren't any cool high school kids there.

We found seats just as the game was getting ready to start. After we sat down Amber started promoting Rusty, not that he needed it. I would not be surprised if Amber has a public relations job in her future.

"Of course, he's on the starting lineup and he's number two." Amber looked for him on the ice. "You know he's won first or second star in every game he's played this series, and pretty much every game he's played since the playoffs started. It must be some sort of record."

A *must see* Rusty. I chuckled to myself.

Rusty skated to center ice and got in line with his team for a warm-up shot.

"There he is!" Amber squealed.

We watched as Rusty literally skated circles around most of his teammates. After the warm-up, both teams got in their positions. It was time for the first face-off. The ref dropped the puck and the game began. Rusty plays center forward. He won the face-off for Glencarter.

The Pirates team colors are black and red. We were playing the Georgetown Screaming Eagles and their colors are white and yellow. Based purely on team colors alone, I think our team has the physical capabilities to get the job done, but the visitors may have more heart.

Amber watched intently, as I enjoyed my fries.

"Amber, do you know where fries were invented?"

"What?" Amber looked surprised at the question. "France?"

"Greece!"

"Really? Huh, I wouldn't have thought that. Rusty has the puck!"

"Amber, it's a joke."

"What?"

"Nevermind."

I kept looking over at Nila. I couldn't help myself. I think I caught her looking at us a couple of times too. Most of the game, she was preoccupied, laughing along with her new friends. Ruby and Beryl were there, with Ava, Kelly, Melissa, and Justine. I saw a few other girls from high school that I didn't know.

One of the most interesting things about going to Glencarter high school next year is that the feeder schools from surrounding districts come together for high school. There are three other schools from rural areas that consolidate into one at the senior high school level. I am looking forward to seeing new people.

The game finished three to one for the Pirates. When the final buzzer rang, the building erupted in cheers. Amber jumped up in excitement with the crowd. Our town may not have many people or much money, but we do have lots of spirit. I saw it fill the rink, with a splendor from all the colors of the rainbow.

After Rusty won the first star of the game, he gave Amber a wink and a wave as they came off the ice.

"Yay! He did it Violet!" Amber exclaimed.

"Yes Amber, they certainly did."

I looked over and saw Nila leaving the rink with Ruby and Beryl by her side.

CHAPTER 26

I spent most of Sunday alone in my room. I was tired, between babysitting Mara and school. As I was dozing to the closing credits of Gilmore Girls on my TV, the phone rang.

"Violet!" Mom yelled up to me. "It's Amber."

I looked at the alarm clock on my nightstand. It was nine o'clock.

"Hello." I tried to sound like I hadn't just woken up.

"Violet, Rusty just called and said there is a nasty rumor going around about me."

Okay, I thought, so what's new?

"A really personal one."

Ah shit. I shook my head awake. I think I know where this is going, I thought. The gossip didn't take long getting back to her. Beads of sweat formed on my forehead and in the palms of my hands.

"Everyone is saying my dad isn't my dad. I never told anyone except for you... *but* we do live in Glencarter, I'm sure someone here remembers him –"

I cut her off, I had to. It was painful listening to her. I had to be honest, I owed her that much and more.

"Amber, I'm sorry, I told Nila about your dad." We were both quiet for a moment. "I know it wasn't my place to say anything and I feel awful. It was the night we went out to The Glen." I nervously bit my bottom lip. "When Nila went to the party at Ava's house, she said, the girls there were talking about it.

"But how would they know?" Amber asked.

"Nila said that Ruby brought it up, she heard it from her mom."

I didn't tell Amber the whole truth. I didn't say the only reason it came up at The Glen was because of the way she talked to me and Nila, or that Nila confirmed it to Ruby and the others at the party. There was no point, none of that mattered now.

I had a hard time taking a breath, I knew Amber felt like she'd been sucker punched, and her knees were weak. I hoped she was sitting down.

"Ruby heard it from her mom!" She repeated the words back to me, sounding pissed and shocked.

"Yes, she knows." Although, I felt bad, it was true. "Ruby's mom lived here at the time. She saw it firsthand. It *is* Glencarter, and everyone knows everyone else's business." I reminded Amber that Ruby really didn't need me or Nila to confirm it.

"You still shouldn't have told Nila! It's nobody business but mine. It seemed like you were trying to pry something out of me that night at your place, and now it's not a secret anymore. You betrayed my trust, Violet." Amber hung up the phone without saying goodbye.

Nila called me early the next morning, it was Monday.

"Violet, I'm not walking to school today. Ruby's dad is going to drive me."

I felt the color drain from my face. "Figures." I hung up the phone without saying goodbye.

I should have saw it coming, Ruby wouldn't want to be associated with kids that *walk* to school. She would shudder at the thought.

I grabbed my school bag and walked outside. I saw the empty path and started to cry. I was losing both of my best friends.

As I walked to school alone, I thought about the drama around me. I hadn't had any dreams for a while. Perhaps the drama interfered with the frequency of my dreams.

Perry and I were becoming closer. We spoke frequently. His life was drama-free, and I liked that, it was more my speed. I appreciated a break from the chaos and the chance to talk about things outside of Glencarter. And I think he appreciated feeling like he was part of the group by hearing what was happening in our lives.

I walked alone to lunch that day, too. When I went into the cafeteria, I saw Nila sitting at Ruby and Beryl's table, and Amber was with Rusty and his friends.

Great! I just love eating alone, I thought, as I took my usual spot at our otherwise empty table. I saw Perry coming from the cash.

"Perry!" I shouted above the bustle of the cafeteria. "Over here." I pointed at the seat beside mine.

His eyes become crescent moons as he smiled, and his aura flashed the color indigo like a flare through the room before white specs moved through it like stars at night.

He smiled awkwardly and rushed toward me. When he sat down at the table, I could tell he was busting at the seams with excitement.

"Violet, why are you all alone?"

I felt like he knew more than he was letting on, I always felt that way with Perry, but I told him everything that happened between Amber and Nila. I figured there was no harm anymore, since almost everyone in the school was talking about it already, anyways. And besides, who would Perry tell?

He acted surprised, "I think she will get over it quickly. I know Amber is pissed now, but she probably won't hold a grudge against you or Nila for long," he tried to reassure me. "This will pass."

"Hopefully you are right, and it's just my guilty conscience getting the best of me, but I wouldn't blame Amber if she never talks to me again," I declared.

"Don't be so hard on yourself, it'll work out." Perry reassured me again, before taking a bite from his hamburger.

We finished our lunches and made plans to eat together again the following day.

"Same time, same place."

"Definitely!" Perry agreed.

That evening, I decided to call Nila. I wanted to try to reason with her. I didn't want to give up on our friendship without a fight.

"Nila, Amber is our best friend. Do you think Ruby cares about you the way Amber does? You're getting dragged into the middle of something that's them. Ruby didn't show interest in you until Amber started seeing Rusty. Couldn't there be a chance she might be using you to try to get back at Amber? Has that ever crossed your mind?" My voice cracked and my eyes filled with tears.

"Violet, Ruby and I are friends now. I'm hanging out with all the other cool kids from high school too. Can't you be happy for me, instead of being jealous?"

What Nila said had a ring of truth to it. Of course, I wanted to be popular, who doesn't but she shouldn't be climbing the social ladder by bringing someone else down, let alone one of her best friends.

Deep down, I knew that even though Nila was choosing Ruby, she was still the same great person and friend that I always loved, despite any mistakes she's making, and the same could be said for Amber.

"Nila, please don't take what I am saying the wrong way. I only want to make peace between you and Amber. I wish you would call her to apologize. I want the three of us to be best friends again and hang out with each other like we used to." I heard Nila crying on the other end of the phone as I let her go, "Good night."

I went to bed shortly after. I said a prayer, hoping that things would get better between Amber, Nila, and me. It couldn't hurt.

Father, giver of all good gifts, I ask you to grant me a favor. If it be in your honor and well-being, please bring me, Amber, and Nila back together, close as ever. Amen.

I drifted off to sleep. I started to dream, and knew I was dreaming. I was on the same street as before. I hadn't been here for several weeks, although it felt like an eternity. I started walking, the street dissolved, and the particles became a brilliant white soft sand under my feet. I was standing on a beach.

The beach ran for miles and miles. It did not end at a horizon, it was infinite. Above me, the sky was a crisp blue. There was not a single cloud in sight. In the center of the sky, in the shape of a perfect circle, was the most beautiful, grandest rainbow I'd ever seen. The colors and the light coming from it were magnificent.

"Violet!"

I looked back down to the beach and Gabriel was standing beside me. It had not been that long since I saw him last, but I'd wondered if we would see each other again. I looked up into his hazel eyes as we embraced. I felt weightless, like I was defying the laws of gravity and floating. My heart began to race, and I felt exhilarated, like I was moving fast with the beats, as my temperature grew warmer.

"Violet," he smiled, "we've been keeping a close eye on you, my dear and you have not let us down. You are exceeding our expectations." He took my hand and we walked together in the sand.

"Let's review your lessons. First, you learned people emit energy, which reveals characteristics about them. This energy is called an aura. Everyone has one and it is represented by one of seven colors. When united, the seven colors become whole, something equivalent to white light."

Gabriel took a deep breath, and his aura became immense. I watched as his energy rolled in waves crashing in the sand around him.

"Violet, your second lesson was about your lucid dreams. They enhanced your study. You knew there was different energy at work, since we are all emitting our own. But, because of your dreams you know a realm where anything you want, or dream, is possible when you set your mind to it, when all the energy there is working together, focused on one goal."

I could feel a burning heat coming up from the shimmering white sand as he spoke, and a superb sun released the same heat down on me from above. I should have been suffering, instead I was filled with a sense of fulfillment and peace.

He continued. "Our third and last lesson is based on biology."

"Like my science classes at school?"

"Yes, exactly! I've followed along to a few of your classes and your teacher, Mr. MacDonald is a hoot."

"He is a very nice man," I agreed, "and he is very informative." I told Gabriel, as if he didn't already know that but I didn't know what else to say.

"Indeed, he is." Gabriel nodded his head. "He's resourceful." Gabriel took another deep breath and his aura became boundless. It had no beginning or end, the waves of energy in his aura no longer broke in the sand around his feet.

"Biology is simply defined as the study of living organisms and their vital processes. The human body is made of many different parts. There are organs, bones, blood, cells and more. Each part of our body, plays a fundamental role." The parts of Gabriel's body lit up as he said them. "When one or more of our parts are damaged, we get sick and depending upon the nature of the sickness, if it gets bad enough, we will die."

"Violet, people's perspectives are changing now because they have to. The transition into your planet's spiritual evolution is necessary to preserve the universe and it has already begun, and you, my dear, will play a major role. People will no longer be living for one person, working for thy self. It will be everyone working for one love, one life. I know that you understand, Violet."

I wanted to say I knew exactly what Gabriel meant and where he was going with this, but I didn't. What was lesson three and how did I fit into it? I didn't say anything because I didn't want to sound stupid. Gabriel saw this and said explained further.

"Violet, there are four primary categories of biology: botany for plants, human biology, microbiology for bacteria, and zoology. But what if I were to tell you that there is a fifth that your planet has not explored yet. The biology of aether."

"Aether?" I'd never heard of it.

"Please pay extra attention to Mr. MacDonald and your biology classes." I watched Gabriel's aura become so bright and emit so much energy that it united with the halo above his head, and then the rainbow in the sky above us. All the energy was as one.

"We are waiting for the secrets of the cosmos to be revealed to your planet. First people must acknowledge their energy as power, then, you must use it according to *The Book of Being*. It is only when these two measures are met that your planet will realign and receive its blessings."

Gabriel's aura grew brighter and brighter until it flashed white, and he was gone. I started walking up the beach by myself. The sand was getting darker and the air colder. I started feeling alone, and even more confused. What could Gabriel have meant? Why did he leave me here alone?

I looked back down the beach in search of Gabriel, he wasn't there. Besides me, the beach was empty. But along the path that Gabriel and I had walked together, I didn't see two sets of footprints in the sand. I counted twelve sets of footprints in total, side by side. We weren't alone as we walked the beach. I found solace in these footprints in the sand, now knowing that we are never truly alone, our loved ones and spirit guides are always with us.

CHAPTER 27

The next morning, I felt more alive than ever before. I sprang out of bed and wrote down everything I remembered from my dream in the spiraled notebook I kept in the nightstand by my bed.

Mom and Dad had left for work already. I checked on Mara, and she was still asleep in her crib. I went back to my room and did a few yoga stretches. I started with a mountain pose into warrior, five-pointed star, forward fold, feet back into downward dog, down into cat position, finishing with child pose. This may be my new routine, I thought.

Afterwards, I went downstairs. Mom had left a note for me on the kitchen counter.

"Violet, I'm sorry but our alarm clock didn't go off this morning. The power must have gone out last night and we slept in. Can you please prepare everything for Mara today? I didn't have time before we left. Love you! Mom."

I put Mara's cereal in a bowl, got her cup ready, and laid her clothes out by the changing table. Mom wouldn't need to get everything ready anymore. I had Mara's requirements down to a tee.

I quickly ate my breakfast, a bowl of Cheerios with toast and jam. Then I went to the bathroom to wash my face and brush my teeth. I was just finishing when Mara awoke.

"Wahhh!" I heard her crying and looked at the clock. It was almost 7:30 a.m. I got her dressed and fed, before I dropped her off at Sue's.

"I got everything ready for Mara this morning." I told Sue. I felt proud.

"Good for you, Violet." I could see that Sue was happy for me.

"I hope I didn't forget anything."

"I'm sure you didn't but don't you worry about that. I'll manage, either way."

"Thanks, Sue!"

I walked toward the path. I didn't expect to see her, but there she was, waiting for me. I grinned from ear to ear when I saw her.

"Oh my God, Nila!" I squealed and ran over to her. "I love you!" I gave her a huge hug, "Did you call Amber?"

"No, I haven't spoken to her yet. I just didn't have the guts to call her," Nila began. "But I did do a lot of soul searching after we talked last night, and maybe you are right about some stuff. When we were in The Glen, Amber hurt my feelings but the more I think about it though, and Amber too… she probably didn't mean any harm by it. She can be unintentionally insensitive, sometimes, and I tend to be *slightly* over-sensitive most times. Especially when it comes from someone I love, like you or Amber."

Blue sparks ignited from Nila's blue aura. True blue, I thought, this comes from her heart.

"Alcohol was involved too, and it seemed to work as a catalyst, magnifying everything. She was just trying to fit in that night too. I don't think she meant to be hateful or hurt us."

Nila looked down as she continued. "Besides, I know what it feels like not to fit in. I didn't mean to leave you out or to make you feel that way either. I'm sorry, Violet."

"Thank you, Nila. I appreciate you saying that, but you don't owe me an apology, I get it."

"Yeah, I have to admit, it was nice hanging out with Ruby and Beryl and being included by the cool kids."

I was filled with a sense of joy. Nila opened herself up to me with such honesty, and her thinking was so grown up. I guess, I am not the only one evolving quickly. We were both maturing in our own ways.

Amber was not waiting for us when we walked into the school together, side by side. We went down the hall to our lockers. Nila's isn't far from mine and Amber's is a couple of classrooms further down the hall.

I opened my locker and a tightly folded note fell out onto the floor in front of me. I picked it up, and almost tore the paper, trying to open it. The writing inside was in red ink, it said, "Thanks for telling everyone about my dad! You're now my ex-best friend gone blabber-mouthing bitch!"

It sounded like what Nila told me the girls were saying about Amber at Ava's party. I remembered the 'ex-best friend gone' reference. And besides, I knew the note wasn't written by Amber. The handwriting was all wrong, too big and pronounced. We have been best friends forever, I knew her handwriting.

"Nila!" I shouted. "Come and see this!" I held up the unfolded note in the air.

She grabbed it from my hand. I watched her scan the paper. She turned three shades of red before she finished. Ruby and Beryl were hanging out with some friends at Beryl's locker, not far behind Nila. They were looking over in our direction with big smirks on their faces. The likes of Ruby and Beryl will never quite understand the bond us three girls share. I'm sure they were shitting their pants when Nila blew her top! She stomped right over to them and squared off with Ruby.

"Now you're bringing Violet into this too!" She crumpled the note tight in her fist. Red sparks flew out from Nila's aura as I saw Amber out of the corner of my eye, up the hall. She was standing in complete shock with Rusty, at his locker, as Nila continued yelling at Ruby. "Who in the hell do you think you are?"

Ruby didn't know what to do. She froze like a deer in headlights. I don't think she ever expected Nila to confront her. She took a step back. "What are you talking about Nila? Why are you defending her?"

"I am defending her, Ruby, because she is my best friend! Do you understand that, or did you forget it?"

Ruby started getting angry. Her eyes narrowed, and red sparks flew out from her aura too. She stepped forward, into Nila's face. She wagged her finger as she shouted.

"Nila, I guess you're trash too, just like your best friend Amber. Didn't your dad leave you too, you big, fat squaw!"

Ruby hit several of Nila's nerves, referencing her dad, her weight and insulting her Mi'kmaq heritage. All hell was about to break loose as big, fat red explosions ignited out from Nila's blue aura, and it was on like *Donkey Kong*.

Nila gave Ruby a shove first.

"Don't hit me, Nila," was the last thing I heard Ruby say before Nila pulled her arm back and slugged Ruby right in her jaw.

Ruby returned the punch, hitting Nila back in the eye. The two exchanged blows as the crowd grew larger around us in a huge circle in the hall.

I lost track of time, but I am sure it was only seconds before Mr. MacDonald and Mr. Lavie broke it up.

Amber and I both ran to Nila's side and in that moment all the anger and the resentment that had built up between us was gone.

Ruby had a bloody lip and Rusty rushed over to her. "Are you okay? I can't believe you got in a fight! You *really* gave it to her!"

Amber saw and heard this, along with everyone else that was standing with us.

"You two," Mr. MacDonald pointed. "Go directly to the principal's office."

Beryl confronted Rusty. "Did you get what you wanted? Are you happy now?" She didn't wait for an answer. She turned around in a huff and marched off to first class while Ruby and Nila walked down the hall.

CHAPTER 28

After the fight, a lot of things changed. Amber called me a couple of nights later.

"You will never guess what I heard today?"

"What?" I replied, even though, I was sure I knew what she was going to say.

"I saw Derek at the grocery store, and he said that Rusty's been spending a lot of time at Ruby's house, hanging out with her older brothers. He'd call there for them and end up talking to *her* most of the time."

"I'm so happy you broke up with Rusty, but it's going to suck seeing them together at school together over the next few weeks."

"Right!"

People were saying that Rusty always liked Ruby. And he only broke up with her because he was trying to get as much tail as he could this year. He definitely didn't want to be a virgin when he started high school. Word is, he didn't think Ruby would be willing *and* he was scared of her brothers.

I'd already heard it all from Nila. She ran into Melissa, one of the high school girls, at the soccer field. She still wants Nila to try out for the basketball team in the fall. She told Nila she admires her ability and team spirit. I agreed with that. They've been keeping in touch, although she hasn't hung out with the high school girls since.

Perry and I had been talking a lot. He pushed and prodded me into telling Amber and Nila about my experiences. He insisted they were ready for it. A few days later, I did.

"You can see what?" Amber asked.

"Auras." I explained them in detail and their meanings.

"Cool!" Nila said. "I wish I could do that!"

"And I found some new friends!" I told them about Seven and Gabriel and my dreams.

"Wow!" Amber said. "I can't believe you have been keeping this to yourself this whole time."

"Well… there is one more thing I have to tell you both." Amber and Nila looked at one another in excitement, anticipating what was next. "I have another new friend that I've been confiding in, someone who actually lives here in Glencarter."

The girls looked surprised, "You do?" Nila asked. "Who is it?"

"It's Perry," I shrugged. The girls looked at each other and back at me, bewildered. "And he's not peculiar, or creepy." Well, he's not creepy in a harmful way, I thought, maybe a talk to the dead sort of way, if you find that sort of stuff creepy.

About a week later, Amber spent the night at my house, and when we were alone, I told her about the red overlay I saw around her aura.

"A red what?"

"An overlay, I'd never heard of it before Seven told me about them." I don't think she was truly in touch with her feelings until I brought it up. "Amber, you must have abandonment issues from your dad." She started speaking more freely about her dad, and her dating after that.

"Violet," she said "I'm not sure what I want. I know that I'm supposed to hate my dad for what he did to my mom and me. But I long to look in his eyes, even if it's just one more time." She turned to me, "Sometimes I do things that aren't right. We all make mistakes, maybe I shouldn't judge him."

I was amazed with Amber. She sounded more mature too. She might have been progressing fastest of the three of us. After we talked, her red overlay was still there, but less prominent than before. She's recovering, but it will take time.

Soon it was mid-June, the last official school day, before exams started. Nila and I were walking to school. "I can't believe this is our last full day of school as junior high students."

"Me either!" I agreed. "Bye-bye, Glencarter Junior High!" I said, feeling more excited than melancholy.

We walked through the main doors into the school. A class of 2002 banner was displayed on the wall in the lobby. Amber and Perry were sitting at the bench, talking while they waited for us to arrive. Nila and I went over and joined them. We hung out for a while before it was time to go to first class.

"I wonder who's going to have a date for the semi-formal?"

"Rusty will bring Ruby." Amber frowned.

We took our seats just before the second bell rang. Because it was the last day, the classroom was a buzz with more excitement than usual. Everyone's auras were beaming. Mrs. Walker took the class roll call. It took longer than normal, she finished with Perry's name. "Perry Van Winkle."

"Present!" Perry said for the class's last time as junior high students.

It was even harder for Mr. MacDonald to settle the biology class down after lunch. Once everyone was quiet, as we could be on the last day, he began.

We were supposed to be reviewing material for exams, but we already finished that. Instead, Mr. MacDonald said he wanted to talk to us about oceans, and how important water is to our planet.

"It was the key ingredient required, after the Big Bang, for life to be formed," Mr. MacDonald said. "The ratio of water on Earth is comparable to the ratio of water or blood in the human body."

It was interesting and I was intrigued. It reminded me of a saying I'd heard before, but the words wouldn't come to me. There was obviously a connection between the body and the Earth in relation to the water ratio, could there be a connection to the colors too? I figured it probably did fit in somewhere.

I was still contemplating what it meant when Mr. MacDonald moved on.

"I went to school in Newfoundland. I am alumni from MUNS University in St John's. A few times during the winter we could see auroras or the northern lights." I noticed how similar the spelling of auroras is to the word auras.

I started thinking about Gabriel. I remembered him saying, "Please pay extra attention to Mr. MacDonald and your biology classes." I knew the information he was passing along to me in this class was important.

CHAPTER 29

That evening, I was lounging around in our living room, waiting for my parents to come home from work. Mara was cranky, and I wanted to be by myself. I was beyond tired.

The last few weeks I'd been busier than ever between school and babysitting. The days were long because my workload was so high, but they also felt short because I never had enough hours to get everything done. I was always tired. At the end of each day, I shook my head in disbelief, wondering where the time had gone.

My parents were about six weeks into the lobster season, and it was taking its toll on all of us. "Look at the mess of that couch." Mom frowned as she walked in.

Really? I thought. It was annoying, I did my best to ensure the house was perfect for her. She seemed to complain a lot lately, no matter what I did, I could not please her.

I know she's tired from working so much, and there is still never enough money, or time. That night, the throw over the couch was a mess, but that was because Mara had just pulled it down.

I straightened it and gave her a hug. "Sorry Mom. Thank you for working so hard for us."

She hugged me back and she started to cry, "You're such a good girl, Violet. Thank you for helping out so much around here. I know you're working overtime.

I'm sorry for snapping at you." Her eyes and aura brightened as we held each other.

That night in bed, I was watching the TV Nan gave me. It was a show we used to watch together, *Buffy the Vampire Slayer*. I was beginning to fall asleep when I heard these words, clear as a bell: "No man is an island."

It startled me awake, I looked around for the source. There was no one else in my room. It was not the TV, though *Buffy* was still on. I turned off the TV to think about the words. I knew the line "no man is an island." It was the quote I was trying to remember in biology class that day.

I wish I had a computer and the internet at home, I thought. I saw Nan's prayer beads hanging from my bed post and remembered what had happened before. I picked them up and held them in my hands.

"Where do I know this quote from?" I repeated the words, "no man is an island."

I immediately knew that the line was from an old poem, and sermon. The author was a metaphysical poet, who was part of the clergy. His name was John Donne and he wrote the poem in 1624. I saw the entire poem in my head.

It began 'No man is an island, entire of itself; every man is a piece of the continent, a part of the main.' It was hard to understand because it was written so long ago. The last paragraph read 'Any man's death diminishes me. Because I am involved in mankind. And therefore never send to know for whom the bell tolls; It tolls for thee.'

Then I saw the meaning of the poem. We, as a planet, are all connected. The poem compares people to a continent. If one person washes away, like a grain of sand, we are all affected by it.

And the final paragraph implies that since we are all connected together, if one of us suffers a loss, we all suffer that same loss.

That's when I had an epiphany – another light bulb moment.

The first few lines from the poem, the ones about an island, made me think of the ratios Mr. MacDonald had been talking about today between water on the Earth and blood in the body being comparable.

If every man is a piece of a continent, so to speak, would it be that far-fetched to say Earth could be part of something that's like a human body.

Gabriel had said that biology is the key. There are five primary types of biology: botany, human, micro, zoology and aether. I was waiting until Monday to look up aether online at school, but now I didn't need to. I clenched Nan's prayer beads in my fist and repeated, what is aether?

I instantly knew that aether is the fifth element in alchemical chemistry and early physics. It is the name given to the material that is believed to fill the universe beyond the terrestrial sphere. The belief in aether as an element was held by medieval alchemists, Greeks, Buddhists, Hindus, Japanese, and the Tibetan Bon.

In simple terms, it is the space and stillness that contains and holds us together. Aether is the element that connects us to our own spirit and intuition, along with other realms and planes.

What if the five types of biology were not so different after all and instead are parts of something greater than we could imagine, like a superhuman or *our* God?

I remembered hearing in church that God created man in his image. What if that was literal? I know human cells are made of atoms, which are protons, neutrons, and electrons. Could our planet be the equivalent to a cell but instead it's made of people, nature, and energy, and the universe is our body.

I had a vision of Mr. MacDonald talking about the northern lights. The purple prayer beads in my hands glowed green. I saw the northern lights through my third eye. The green waves moved with the stars shimmering and shifting behind them during the night. It resembled the way I see someone's energy. Could these lights be the equivalent to an aura but on a much grander scale, say Godly? The scientific name is aurora borealis.

And if all of this is true, what about the Big Bang? I had my own theory about that now.

We took sex ed in grade 7 health class and if everything else is true, the Big Bang sounds like it could be the equivalent to the moment of conception?

I've heard that a person's hair color and disposition are predetermined before birth through their DNA. So, in that moment, when we are created, we are complete. If the Big Bang was the moment of conception, instead of expanding over time, we have actually been growing.

From the moment of conception, or the Big Bang, we have been changing. First, we became the equivalent to a zygote, then blastocyst, followed by an embryo, and a fetus before becoming a baby, like Mara! Soon she will be a toddler, preschooler, grade-schooler, middle-schooler or pre-teen, teenager, then adult, followed by middle aged and if lucky enough, a senior before an impending death.

I closed my eyes, my mind stopped, and everything
was black. Stars appeared and started speeding past me.
I heard Mr. MacDonald's voice. He was reviewing one
of our biology classes. It was his lecture on the Big
Bang Theory and he was talking about matter versus
anti-matter. The stars I saw moving started making
structures and they turned into his classroom. I had a
vision of the biology class from that day, as I continued
listening to him.

"These two components, you see class, are complete
opposites of one another and when they meet, they
cancel each other out."

It was then that another dimension to this concept
was brought forth in my mind. It was Gabriel's third
lesson: By being components of the universe itself, we
are also key components of matter *and* anti-matter!

My conclusion is that both positive and negative
people and energy exist. Some might even call them,
good and evil. Would it be far-fetched to say that
maybe time was created to give the negative people an
opportunity to change? We are evolving to a point
where only positive people exist.

I think that there has always been more positive on
the planet than negative, right from the very beginning
of time. There has always been good and evil on Earth,
and the good always seems to outweigh the bad.

The positive people are leading us into this new era.
As time goes by, the ratio of positive people will grow,
until a time comes when we are only left with
positivity. The negativity will eventually become
positive or die out.

I am not saying we will no longer be individuals.
The negative people will have the same choices they
always had. They'll continue on the same paths or see

the error of their ways and redeem themselves. We shouldn't try to push them. It's much greater than that. They have the right to redemption. It is part of their covenant and our own.

People have the choice to become something positive and the way we can help most is by being living examples. I showed a fly that was buzzing around my bedroom window the way outside. The key is to remember that lots of little things do add up to *big* things and a *big* difference over time.

Once the negativity is gone, we as an entity will be healed. Until then, our planet is like a cancer cell, both infecting our God's body and preventing our people's dreams from becoming our truth.

We are all striving toward one functioning mind, body and soul, whether we realize it or not. When we are in tune with the rest of the universe, working together, we will inherit the greatest gift of all – and it will be the equivalent of white light.

I sighed and smiled as my energy became in sync with the energy frequency around me. I turned into my covers and settled into sleep for the night.

CHAPTER 30

Semi-formal had arrived. I was happy it was here, but a little sad at the same time that junior high was almost over. We were psyched about high school next year and what the future might bring, but I felt like I was leaving part of myself behind tonight, maybe my childhood. We were growing up fast and I wasn't sure I was ready for it.

Nila and I went to Amber's house before the dance. She had everything a girl could ever ask for when it came to cosmetics and accessories. My parents didn't take the night off work. Semi-formal was not as big as prom, but they did ask Sue to watch Mara. We were looking forward to our last night out together as junior high students.

Perry had become part of our lives. We were going to pick him up on the way to the restaurant. He was going to eat with us before the dance. We were having supper at The Five Fisherman, the only fancy restaurant in Glencarter. We had a table reserved for the four of us. It is a junior high school tradition for graduates. Almost everyone from our class will be there.

We were doing finishing touches to our hair and makeup before it was time to leave. I couldn't find my lip gloss anywhere.

"Why?" I cried out in frustration. "Where is it?"

I found myself going back to something I picked up in a book after Gabriel referenced angels in one of our dreams.

Angels and spirit guides, please help me find my missing lipstick. I repeated it in my head three times. It may sound simple and silly, but it works. The item usually shows up within a few minutes, and that night was no exception.

I saw the cover of it almost immediately out of the corner of my eye. It had slid underneath Amber's vanity. Thanks, I thought, I reached down for it, applied the color to my lips and smacked them together when I was done.

We checked ourselves in the mirror one last time before leaving. Amber was wearing her hair down, except for a few braids around her face, which she set with bobby pins. Her blonde curls bounced with her. She had on a short light-yellow dress, and bright pink pumps.

Nila always had great hair. That night, she had hers up and it was embellished with blue colored baby's breath. She was wearing a baby blue empire waist dress that almost touched the floor.

Amber had helped me curl my hair, and she set it in place with pins. I wore a purple satin dress that flared at the waist. I didn't feel plain, like I usually did.

"You both look gorgeous tonight," I said.

"Thank you!" Amber replied.

"You look awesome too!" Nila said, with a huge smile on her face.

We were beaming like beacons in the night.

Amber's dad was driving us, as usual. He picked up Perry on the way. He looked handsome in his crisp white shirt and black pants. He had an indigo bow tie too.

How fitting, I thought.

I felt nostalgic as we drove to The Five Fisherman. It was our last supper as junior high students. I knew that the future was infinite, but I was going to miss this. I looked at Amber's dad. He looked better than normal. Amber had told me that he cut back on his drinking.

The walls inside the restaurant had a high gloss wooden finish and the tablecloths were our school colors, maroon and yellow. The same colors also adorned almost every available spot in the restaurant. It made us feel special.

"You did a fantastic job decorating tonight," I said, to the pretty, brown-eyed waitress as she guided us to our seats.

"Thank you so much! We really tried." Her aura brightened and I sensed she was excited about her own senior prom the following week. "Here are your menus." She passed them around the table.

We had our choice of beef, chicken, and fish dishes. Each of us ended up ordering the chicken fingers with fries and vegetables. Maybe we were not *that* grown up yet.

When we got to the school, I could feel the energy outside coming from inside of the school.

"Thanks again for the drive, Mr. Boertien." I said, as we got out of the vehicle. Nila and Perry thanked him too.

"Have fun girls, and you too Perry!"

I was worried Amber might be sad about going alone after thinking Rusty would be her date, but I could tell when we walked in that she was happy to be there with us. Her aura was exceptional! It was big, bright, and sparkly. I could barely see her red overlay.

When we walked inside, a handful of grade 8 students met us at the door.

"Tickets, please." We handed them the paper tickets we received from the school spirit committee.

The cafeteria floor was full of kids. The grade eight students were allowed to come to the dance, along with us. The younger grade decorates for the dance. It's a school tradition and they did a wonderful job. The room was filled with tons of dollar store imitation candles and some spring flowers. They were the same colors as a rainbow. I could rhyme them off by heart: red, orange, yellow, green, blue, indigo, and violet. I thought about Gabriel and Seven. The cafeteria reminded me of what I imagine heaven will look like.

Almost everyone was wearing at least one piece of clothing that was the same color as their aura. For the girls, it was their dress or corsage. For the guys, it was mostly their ties. Except for Alex, he was wearing a red bandanna on his head. He looked like a pirate, and it suited him. He's the only person I know who could pull it off, too. He stood out in the crowd, not that it was unusual for him.

The DJ was playing pop music, mostly the songs I heard on the radio during the *Top Nine at Nine*, along with the occasional classic rock song. Strobe lights lit the room and circled the white walls, the room was engulfed in a sea of colors from the crowd's clothing and their auras. The lights were the same colors as my dreams.

I was surprised when I heard a slow song start early in the evening. I didn't recognize it at first, maybe because it was so out of place. As soon as I did, my eyes met Perry's. It was "Over the Rainbow" from *The Wizard of Oz*.

Perry walked to me, and he took my hand. I looked up, into his eyes, deep into those dark green eyes…

"Would you care to join me?" he asked.

I think he was half joking when he said it, but I accepted just the same. We walked onto the dance floor, as our auras dazzled shimmering in the lights.

Perry pulled me in when we got on the dance floor and sparks flew as we began to dance. I could feel the electricity between us. It may sound corny, but we were captivated by one another as we circled together on the floor. I closed my eyes and lost track of time as we turned. I looked up at the large, oversized clock hanging high on the cafeteria wall. It showed eight-twenty, but the second hand was *not* moving. Time stood still and our night was only beginning.

Rusty and Ruby were beside us, partly dancing, but mostly slobbering over each other. They must have had drinks before the dance, or snuck some booze in, or both, I thought.

Ruby was wearing a long light red dress that flowed with her as she moved. Her hair was in a bun on the crown of her head. It was accentuated with white jewels that circled around its base. Rusty had given her a white, red, and orange colored corsage. He was wearing an orange and red tie. It would have been better for the fall, but the colors really suited them.

They looked great, but they were louder than usual, especially Rusty, and they were getting attention for all the wrong reasons. Their auras looked small, dark, and murky.

As Perry and I danced, I thought about how the night was marking an end of an era for everyone here – not only was winter over, but the grade was also over, and junior high was over too. Time's an important factor in our lives. Everything changes in time, and we are no exception to that.

I lifted my head from Perry's shoulder and the cafeteria changed too. It was brighter, and it grew brighter and brighter with our auras as the crowd danced in circles until we couldn't tell one from another. Our energy shifted and shimmered intertwining together as we danced. The intensity of our auras grew brighter and brighter until we united, and the room flashed white.

I whispered to Perry, "We are already in closer harmony with one another than I could have dreamed possible."

Perry held me tighter and as we danced blue sparks ignited like lightening from both of us. Off in the distance, in another realm, I could hear Nan, Gabriel, Seven, and others cheering together from somewhere over the rainbow as the song faded into the night.